CLICKED

PATRICK JONES

Clicked
ISBN # 978-1-78651-878-1
©Copyright Patrick Jones 2016
Cover Art by Posh Gosh ©Copyright March 2016
Interior text design by Claire Siemaszkiewicz
Finch Books

Published in 2016 by Finch Books Newland House, The Point, Weaver Road, Lincoln, LN6 3QN, United Kingdom.

CLICKED

Dedication

Thanks to Andrew K., Carrie M., Chloe W., Mark M. and Mollie W., who read this manuscript and provided invaluable feedback. Thanks to Judy Klein for her copyediting wizardry and, as always, thanks to Erica Klein, for her support. Finally, with thanks and praise to the late, great Warren Zevon, whose song titles I pinched for story titles in this book.

Author's Note

"Satire and parody are important forms of political commentary that rely on blurring the line between truth and outrageousness to attack, scorn and ridicule public figures. Although they may be offensive and intentionally injurious, these statements contain constitutionally protected ideas and opinions, provided a reasonable reader would not mistake the statements as describing actual facts" — Reporters Committee for Freedom of the Press

Prologue

Christmas morning
Almost three years earlier

My sister Caitlin screams — I can hear her all the way up in my room on the second floor.

She stayed out all night, again. Now, she's back in the house and the endless arguments within my family, mostly between Dad and Caitlin, rage. It's another battle in their ongoing war, but I seem to be the only casualty.

Once Dad stops, Mom takes over. I leave my room and move to the top of the stairs.

"We were so worried," Mom says. Her words bounce around the high ceilings.

"Don't lie to me," Caitlin shouts back. "Nobody in this house cares about me."

I want to shout from the top of stairs, 'I care, Caitlin. I love you!', but say nothing.

"What's this morning's melodrama, Caitlin?" Carol asks. The contempt in her voice rises like stench from the garbage. Unlike me, who tries to clutch onto Caitlin as she slips away, Carol kicks her to the curb.

"If you want to stay here, you're going to do things our way!" Dad yells. He's shorter than me, only five eight to my six one, but he yells with the fury of a man over seven feet tall.

"I'm not perfect like Carol. I'm just a fuck-up!" Caitlin shouts. "So I do what I want and there's nothing any of you can—"

Dad cuts her off. "You need to leave now. That's enough. Caitlin, you need to leave."

Loud. Firm. Final.

"Tossing your daughter out on Christmas," Caitlin says.

"Your actions, your consequences," Mom says.

"I messed up. I want a second chance," Caitlin says.

"You've used up your second chances," Mom says.

And now Mom and Caitlin are at it, with Carol adding snide comments like a dog lifting his leg. "Seriously, Caitlin, you are such a cliché—the messed up middle child, I mean—"

"And that's what I hate the most!" Caitlin shouts back. And it's on between the sisters.

"I can't live like this anymore," Dad says, his words fading, followed by heavy footsteps.

"Daddy, where are you going?" Caitlin shouts. More steps, a door opens, closes.

"Caitlin, we ground you. You ignore it," Mom says. "We show we love you and you look at us with such hate. I don't know what else we can do since you won't change."

Caitlin mumbles something in return. I hope they are words that save her, save us.

"If we can't love you or control you, then we can't have you live here," Mom says.

"I'm so sorry, for everything," Caitlin says, I think through tears. "This time I will change."

"But you don't change. You say you will and you don't," Mom says. "There are —"

But her words are cut short by the sound of the door opening then heavy footsteps. Dad's probably back. It's his last chance to say something or do something to save his family, but the only noises are shouts from the women. Mom's the loudest.

"Oh my God, James, no," Mom yells. "What in God's name are you thinking?"

"Daddy, what are you doing?" Caitlin asks. Carol yells something similar.

"Caitlin, here's my pistol. Take it from me," Dad says in a stone cold voice. "We can't live with you out of control like this. Take the gun and end this! Either kill yourself or kill us."

Then there's silence for ten seconds.

I hear nothing except the beating of my heart.

Twenty seconds.

I want to run downstairs, save my family, but I'm frozen in the heat of the moment.

Thirty seconds.

The silence of a life and death decision is the loudest sound in the universe.

Finally Caitlin screams, "I hate you," and there's the metallic clicking sound of a trigger against an empty chamber. I hear the sounds, I can't see the faces. I can only hear questions spinning in my head one after another. Who was Caitlin speaking to? Who held the gun? Did that person know the gun wasn't loaded? Who pulled the trigger? Where was the gun pointed?

Seconds later I hear another loud clicking sound — that of Caitlin's always high heels against the hard floor. A door slams, and I worry I'll never see the sister I love so much again.

Chapter One

Friday, October 8th
Evening of Fenton High homecoming football game

"Welcome home, Carson," Dad says as I walk in the front door.

I mumble a non-response, then quickly scale the family photo-free stairs as my head spins with the simple significance of that compound word— homecoming.

Homecoming is no ordinary word. I should know because as a future bestselling, award-winning novelist, I'm good with words. Tonight, homecoming means the football game that I watched to report on for my school paper. Tomorrow will be the homecoming dance, which I won't attend. I'm glad not to be attending a school dance, thanks to my prom fiasco with Thien. As I walk up toward my room, I'm not thinking about last spring's prom, but of that Christmas morning when Caitlin ran away.

Every morning I Google her name, 'Caitlin Banks', but she remains a mystery, like a haunting memory or elusive mirage. My parents gave up searching, mentioning her name and even having her photos in the house. I pray they still have hope. I do.

In seconds my dependable four-year-old MacBook Pro comes on and I start clicking away at the keyboard and mouse, the sound echoing in silence. I see on the screen that I'm not the only one in front of a computer instead of a keg. It looks like many of my friends — National Honor Society all-stars and newspaper nerds — are online as well. I chat to fight the loneliness that a weekend like this magnifies a million times. Finishing the football story for the paper comes easily, so I quickly transition into the online pursuit of seventeen-year-old boys everywhere. Every time I look at porn I feel guilty, but I'm not sure why. It's free. It's exciting, and nobody gets hurt. Besides, one-hand fantasies and wet dreams are the extent of my sex life. Given how things ended with Thien at the prom, that's probably just as well for me and all Fenton High girls.

I sit alone in my room in my parents' soon-to-be-foreclosed-on house in suburban Flint, Michigan, surfing worldwide porn when I see a thumbnail of a white guy and a black guy, between them a young blonde girl with nice, natural tits. I click the image. The picture gets larger while my world grows smaller. The naked blonde girl on the screen is my sister Caitlin.

Chapter Two

Saturday, October 9th
Morning of Fenton High homecoming dance

"Good morning, sunshine," Dad says. It's ten in the morning. He's been up for hours. He sounds as bitter as the coffee grounds he's pouring hot water through, probably for the fourth time. He runs his hand through his gray hair. He'll dye it brown if he ever gets a job interview. It's been months.

I yawn, rub my eyes and say nothing. The anger passes quickly. If I had a life like Dad then lost it through forces I couldn't control, maybe sarcasm would be the only thing I'd have left too.

"What are you doing today?" Dad asks in a tone that implies I'd better have a good answer.

I reach for cereal. I can't say, *Same thing I did until six in the morning, you know, looking for porn pictures of my sister, your daughter.* I can't say it because it's cruel, and because I couldn't find any more in the thousand other

13

pix and vids I explored. There was only one set of stills of her from the *Homemade Hos #115* DVD. I found the web page of the company who produced it and sent an email asking how to contact the actress in the interracial threesome.

"You deaf like Grandpa Chuck?" Dad asks. "Except you don't have the excuse. You didn't hang hoods in a GM plant for thirty years. So, what are you doing to do today, Carson?"

I hate when Dad gets like this, all in my face. He's not mad at me. He's just angry. Bored. Out of work two years now and going on forever.

"Looking for a job." But not right away since I look like hell. My light brown-almost-blond hair sits flat rather than turned up in front and my pathetic attempt at a beard remains stunted, both desperate attempts to attract the attention of actual females.

Dad laughs, a big, hearty yet totally fake laugh. "Good luck with that."

I fill a cereal bowl with knock-off corn flakes and shovel them into my mouth without milk so I can stop this conversation before I say something mean. I need to find a job because I need money. I always need money but now it's essential. If—I mean when—I find Caitlin, I'll bring her home. I'll save her from the life she's fallen into somehow. I doubt she's in Michigan—probably LA or Vegas, the porn capitals of the United States. That means I'll need travel cash.

Mom walks in the room. She's dressed up for work, not that she brings in much money. She observes the out of place, bemused look on Dad's face and smiles. "What's so funny?"

"Carson says he wants to get a job," Dad says. Another fake laugh.

Mom frowns. "If you need money," Mom says, but stops. There's no money. The auto industry collapse and the human cyclone Caitlin took it all. Parts of the auto industry bounced back, but for older workers like Dad, it left nothing but tread marks. Mom wears her 'I'll sell a house today' smile, a bright yellow dress to match her fake blonde hair and faker gold jewelry.

"No, I need a job." I walk over to make myself some coffee. A tall, skinny and wired guy like me needs caffeine like Superman needs steroids, but I'm hooked on the rush.

"We're working on a way to pay for college," Dad says. If there's money, and that's an elephant-sized if, he wants me to attend the engineering program at Michigan Tech in the Upper Peninsula. If not, and if I can get in—another elephant—he'll settle for Kettering in Flint, but he doesn't like the 'changing' neighborhood, which is code for black. I don't share my dreams of going to Princeton like my hero F. Scott Fitzgerald or to a small liberal arts school like Oberlin with a strong creative writing program.

"This isn't about college," I say. "It's about earning money for myself, not from you."

"It might be hard to find a job," Mom says. She's sympathetic. She's knowledgeable about finding jobs. In the almost eighteen years of my life, Mom's had six careers and ten jobs—or is it six jobs and ten careers? She thinks each one is going to be the dream job that makes us rich. Mom's as delusional as suckers playing the lottery or selling Amway crap.

"If you work, then I assume you'll take over car expenses," Dad says then sips his coffee.

I reply the same, stalling. He's trying to sound tough, fatherly, but it fails him. They treat me like this delicate thing, afraid I might break. My parents used to be strict. That worked with Carol, backfired with Caitlin. The jury's out on how it will work with me, their youngest child. The oldest, Carol, was the dream child—Miss Homecoming Queen Honor Roll Student Council. Then on the Boston College Dean's list and now in San Diego working for a big software company. Second child, the troubled middle one, Caitlin Autumn Banks. A failure, a parent's nightmare. On the road to becoming a Carol clone until tenth grade when the cyclone of her chaos blew into our lives. I'm the tiebreaker—my parents' fates, as parents, hang in the balance of my life.

"We had a deal about car expenses." I push back. I hate to lie or argue with my parents. They need no grief given what Caitlin put them through, especially her aborted senior year.

"Maybe we need a new deal," Dad says.

"Thank you, FDR," I joke, but he doesn't laugh. Our deal is they count my being active in things, like newspaper or the new creative writing club that I helped form, as working. Every hour I put into school activities, they pay me—far under minimum wage—to fund expenses related to driving Mom's more rust than gray Malibu. That's also Caitlin's legacy. Caitlin never attached herself to any club at school, just the wrong cliques and worse boys, then older men.

"Why do you need money?" Mom asks, trying not to sound too concerned, so as not to surrender her upbeat salesperson charade. It's Saturday and she's off to sell houses in Flint, which is like trying to sell Bibles at Mecca. If she wants to sell houses, then maybe she could start with ours before the bank takes it away. "Are you in some sort of trouble?" Mom used to be cheerful but Caitlin took Mom's joy with her when she walked out of the door.

"Mom, everything's fine."

She smiles and swallows the biggest lie I've ever told.

Over omelets, we continue the eggshell conversations, my parents interested and concerned, but trying not to push too hard. Me, desperately wanting to tell them the truth, or even a part of it, but instead showing them mercy. By the end of breakfast it's resolved that before she goes to work, Mom will take me to Target to buy interview outfits. I'll start applying for jobs and they'll stop asking me why. Given that all Caitlin did was suck money out of the house, you'd think they'd be happy with me bringing some in, but I know it's not about that. They want—no, they *need*—me reliant on them so they still have a purpose as parents. But I know I can't depend on them for this task. I need to find Caitlin without their knowledge or help.

After breakfast, as I walk up the stairs, I remember all the times I got sent to my room when my parents had it out with Caitlin. Even if I told my parents what I saw last night online, I'm not sure it would do any good. They'd be relieved to find out she was alive, but I just know they couldn't bring her home, especially given her last words from her lips—'*I hate you*'—and what I guess was her last action with Dad's gun, *click*.

Chapter Three

Saturday, October 9th
Evening of Fenton High homecoming dance

I thought I'd found more pix of Caitlin on the Homegrown Video site, but it was this blonde with bad fake tits. She was hot, and soon so was I, until I clicked on the last photo showing the girl's cum-covered face. A bone-chilling thought shot through me. All these girls are some father's daughter, somebody else's sister and some other family's nightmare come true. Is there some other seventeen-year-old boy somewhere in the world finding his sister on a porn site? Given the seemingly infinite universe of porn, it is most likely I'm not the only one feeling a wave of emotions as I watch a loved one having sex — not to share personal intimacy, but for impersonal entertainment and erotic excitement.

Yet, finding Caitlin on a porn site falls into the shocked but not totally surprised category. Unskilled in sports, untalented in the arts and uninterested in school, the one thing Caitlin always had going for her was physical self. A cute middle child who craved attention from anyone, as she got older, she used her body to get noticed by boys. This hit home the summer before seventh grade, when Caitlin was about to start her sophomore year. My fellow non-jock friends like Kevin Baker began summer in my room shooting aliens on video games. On the first super-hot day, we headed to our back yard pool — which now sits empty — only to find Caitlin there tanning. I'd tried not to notice but it was hard not to miss how Caitlin had quickly transformed from flat-chested to filled out. She did nothing to conceal that fact either.

After that, whenever my friends came over to the house, the guys would head to the pool if Caitlin was around. They'd noticed Caitlin in a big way, but she'd noticed them, too. In a few days, she went from ignoring us to making herself the center of attention. A red thong bikini, a fondness for walking in front of my friends on endless non-existent errands and a newfound enthusiasm for pool volleyball did the trick. For years she'd lived in Carol's shadow, but now in the bright sunlight, she shone on her own, for the world — or at least my friends — to see.

"Carson! It's time to go!" Mom yells. They're dropping me at First Wok, where my best pal Tim works, on their way to Saturday mass at Holy Family. My parents were never devout, just Easter and Christmas Catholics, but Caitlin changed that, too. They re-embraced religion when Caitlin started breaking bad. Like if she didn't change, then it was God's fault, not theirs.

At First Wok, I glom a free meal, drink coffee and hang out with Tim in between customers, the few there are. I watch him wait tables. He watches me scribble in my notebook. The sweetest sound in the world is when an exciting idea comes and I click the pen so words flow like the endless refills of coffee Tim pours in my cup. Truth is, I'm not even writing. I'm just transposing the dream movie from my mind to paper. I never wanted a tablet or laptop. There's something satisfying about the rubbing of pen against paper that no computer can match. Friction creates the best fiction in so many ways.

Near the end of his shift, Tim sits at the table with me. He's a math machine, but he doesn't need mad skills to add up the few tip dollars he earned tonight. Just like the stores I visited to apply for work without any success since nobody in Flint is hiring teens this fall, First Wok's business is dying with everything else in Fenton, in Michigan. I can almost feel the squeeze of my mitten-shaped state shrinking.

"You think your uncle could give me a job here?" I don't look up when I ask.

"Carson, dude, I don't think so, but I'll ask him," Tim replies.

"I'll do anything. Wash dishes, bus tables, whatever."

"I thought you wanted to be a writer, not a waiter?" He wipes his wire-rimmed glasses clean. "I wish you had my job, but I wish for lots of things. Should I name my want list for you?"

I chuckle. Tim, like me, is alone on homecoming. Most of our male friends are more adept at calculating a hypotenuse than hooking up. Given the male to female ratio in math and science AP classes, guys like Tim analyze the odds of coupling and know better than to expend the effort. "It'll make a great story to tell your kids, Tim—when you're rich—about the value of hard work."

"Maybe," Tim says. That Tim will be successful and live that American dream is all but certain. He's a lock for schools that Dad wouldn't imagine that I could get into, like MIT or Carnegie Mellon. We'll both apply to Princeton, but my chances of getting in, let alone affording that school, are less than zero. Tim's got a leg-up on that ladder off this rocky ground.

"Thanks, Tiny Tim Wang," I crack.

"You're welcome, Big Carson Penis," he says, per usual. How was his family to know one hundred and fifty years ago when they arrived as Chinese immigrants in California that 'Wang' would take on a different meaning, especially in the immature universe of guys like us? Although, as I know from the monster cocks of porn, I'm Average Size Carson, at best.

"Well, ask him, okay?" I say softly. I hate asking friends for favors, especially Tim, and not only because he's never ever asked me for any favor for any reason. One of the last of many favors I asked was to help set me up with Thien last spring, but that totally backfired. Tim still goes to Honor Society meetings, but I'm NHS non grata. Thien avoids me like the plague I am.

"But a job would put such a crimp in your social life," he cracks.

"My social life is watching you spill soup," I counter. "What am I clinging to?"

He laughs. We met in ninth grade, during gym, as we battled over who would *not* be the last one for whatever teams were forming. Tim always got picked last because he's never met a meal that he didn't like or finish. I got picked next to last because I'm just clumsy, which I blame on the Banks growth spurt curse. Carol grew from adorable to attractive overnight, while I leaped from short and skilled to tall and awkward between eighth and ninth grade. Caitlin's growth spurt took her from A-cup to C-cup in one summer. With how Caitlin showed off in every online photo and YouTube vid, it was really a 'see-me' cup. Once Caitlin ran, my junior high friends like Kevin stopped hanging out, and Tim fell into the open slot. Senior year upon us, we're still best friends.

"I'd need off the third Thursday of every month, when the creative writing club meets."

"How's that club going?" The first meeting was three weeks ago, but Tim's been so busy with work, studying and college stuff that we've had no time to talk other than occasional IMs.

"You're looking at the new vice president of the Fenton High creative writing club!" I say with mock pride to overshadow my disappointment. You always shout the big lie.

"Vice President? So who's president?"

"Josh Brown," I sigh. "Don't worry. I'm making plans."

"Assassination," Tim says, very seriously, which is very funny.

"I'd do it, except I don't want people to know my middle name. It seems the only people you know the middle names of are those who follow in the tradition of assassins like John Wilkes Booth or Lee Harvey Oswald," I say.

Tim laughs. It echoes in the almost empty restaurant. "What is your middle name?"

"Danger," I reply.

He laughs again, like he would at my real middle name — August.

"Carson Danger Banks — if that is your real name — I'll keep your secret safe," Tim says. Part of me wants to ease in with *speaking of secrets,* but I'm not ready to reveal what I learned about Caitlin to Tim. Porn's everywhere, yet it's also oddly private. "But, dude, I don't understand."

"Understand what?"

"Understand how they couldn't elect you president, it was your idea. That's so unfair."

"No, that's high school." Another laugh.

"Do you know why Josh is even back in school?" Tim asks. Josh had been at a private school the past three years, but re-emerged for his senior year at Fenton.

"Maybe it's the Second Coming. The weather calls for cloudy skies with a chance of Four Horsemen," I crack. "I'd ask Josh, but doubt he'd stoop so low as to talk to someone like me."

"Carson, relax, he's just a person," Tim says before he waits on a rare customer, leaving me with my twisted thoughts. Josh isn't just a person any more than Gatsby is just a guy who Nick knows. I don't know Josh well enough to hate him as a person. It's the idea of him that angers me. He's everything I dream of being, yet deep down doubt that I'll ever achieve.

Chapter Four

Monday, October 11ᵗʰ

"How'd the job hunt go?" Dad asks when I walk in the door. He's sitting where I left him a few hours ago — in the living room, watching ESPN while solving a newspaper crossword during the commercials. Dad used to look at the want ads in the paper, but he's abandoned that hopeless pursuit. I say nothing, but my discouraged face tells the story of my job search.

"Welcome to my world," he shouts over the TV.

"Just not many jobs in Fenton for the world's second most promising young writer," I crack. Josh Brown, of course, has never and will never work a hard day in his privileged life.

Dad shrugs and puts down the paper. "Who's the first?"

"Josh Brown," I respond, then tell Dad the story about Josh's return to FHS.

"How can I become a great writer if I can't even be the best at crappy Fenton High?"

"You should think about something more practical, Carson. Learn a trade."

"And that worked out so well for you," says his asshole ungrateful son.

He sips his coffee, which is cold, and says nothing, which is colder.

Dad planned to start college, but Mom got pregnant with Carol, so he went to work on the line at GM Truck Assembly. He'd work a while, get laid off, get called back. After a few years of this, soon after Caitlin was born, he started going back to school to learn a trade. By the time I was born, he'd moved off the line and become a pipefitter. He made enough money that we could afford to move from Flint into Fenton. Things were good, but then that job started the same pattern— work some, get laid off, work some more. When Carol was in high school, Dad went back to school a second time and started all over in machine repair, which he always said was the best job in the plant. Nothing but problem solving all day, and no matter what happens, they'll always need machine repairmen—or so he thought. But then the economy tanked again. He was laid off, except this last time was maybe *the* last time.

"Sorry, Dad, that was mean," I confess.

"Don't know how to break it to you, son, but no matter who you are or what you do," he says slowly, trying to sound wise, "there's always going to be someone better at it than you."

"Wow, Dad, thanks for the pep talk. You should apply for a job as a football coach!"

He sips more coffee. "Son, I'm just telling you how the world works. Take or leave it."

"Is that what you and Mom told Caitlin? That she wouldn't make it?" I snap in anger.

Dad gulps the coffee since I've broken the unwritten rule of the Banks household. Don't talk about Caitlin, don't even mention her name. I know some of the other things he said to her — *'We can't live with what you've done and what you've become. Take it and end this!'* — so nothing would surprise me. The trauma of that Christmas morning shook all shock out of me.

The real question I want to ask, but never can, is what happened that morning. But they don't know I heard it all. Dad doesn't know how much the choice he gave Caitlin haunts me still.

Dad stares at me for a second, not angry or hurt — more confused. After a few seconds, he rises from his chair. He taps me on the arm as he passes by me. "Come outside with me." He walks into the kitchen, places the coffee cup in the sink and heads toward the door. Do I follow his orders — that worked for Carol — or defy him like Caitlin? Which sister am I most like? I follow him into the kitchen, but that's as far as I can make my body move.

"I got stuff to do," I say. "I need to get something ready for creative writing club."

"Seems like you already made up your mind that you're not the best, so why bother?"

I hate when Dad, or anyone, calls me on my self-hating bullshit. Why can't they let me whine and wallow in my envy and anger? It's a space Caitlin and I shared too often.

"Unlike those crossword puzzles I do, the world's not black and white," Dad says. He puts on his work jacket and opens the door. "But maybe, Carson, you already know everything."

He closes the door behind him and I stand in the kitchen. Here's what I do know — not just about Dad and his lost American dream, not just about Caitlin's lust for fame and her lack of talent, not just about Mom's plans to strike it rich with some new career. Like my goal of being the best writer at school, like all those expectations people build up around high-school milestones like homecoming and prom, around holidays, Thanksgiving and Christmas, it seems high hopes just set up bitter disappointment. I don't need Tim's talent with trigonometry to figure out this simple equation— Despair measures the distance between daily life and dreams.

"You coming or not?" Dad shouts. I look out of the window. It's cold for October and I can see his breath. He opens the garage and ducks out of sight. He's challenging me to decide if I want to be the good son or the bad son. You'd think after that test failed so badly with Caitlin on Christmas morning, he'd never, ever ask one of his kids to make that choice again.

I head upstairs, turn on the computer, sit down, but there's nothing but a blank screen.

Despite my daily no-porn pledge, I head straight for skin sites. I block out the knowledge, not just of Caitlin, but that any of these girls are real. They're props, not people. I know from Thien that real people — at least any real girl I'm likely to meet — are nothing like these girls on the screen. Real girls, in my limited experience, don't shout your name, scream in ecstasy or do the sexual things like porn chicks. Like most lessons, I learned that one the hard way.

I stop when I see another blonde with big tits. Not Caitlin, but it could be. How can I keep doing this?

How can I keep looking at this knowing my sister is doing this — or worse?

Unable to look at the sadness of porn or the horror of the empty screen, I do what I should've done in the first place. I put on my hoodie and head outside to be with Dad.

He's in the garage, cleaning the snowblower. "What are you doing? It's October!"

"I like to be prepared." That's Dad to a T, which might explain why we're still in this house. Dad's a big saver, I would say. Frugal, Mom would say. A cheap bastard, Caitlin said.

As we work on the snowblower, we talk about nonsense like Detroit sports and school, certainly not about Caitlin. He deals with the insides, changing spark plugs and the like, while I work on the chute and auger. When I reattach the snowblower discharge chute, it makes a clicking sound.

"You know what that means?" Dad asks.

"No, what?"

"That the work is good and the parts fit together perfectly," he continues. "Too loose, no click. Too tight, no click, just lots of cracking. But that clicking sound means it is just right."

"Are you Goldilocks or Mr. Goodwrench?" I ask.

He laughs again. Dad doesn't laugh much anymore, and if I were him, I'd feel the same. He's lost his job, one of his daughters and he's hanging on to his house by his grease-stained fingertips. My dad can fix about any machine or finish any crossword, but he can't repair his broken family or his busted American dream. His life has sometimes been too hard and for a while, maybe too soft. One day soon — the day that I bring

Caitlin home to him — maybe Dad's life will be just right.

Chapter Five

Friday, October 15th
Publication day

"Is everybody fired up about publication day?" Mr. Jakes, our journalism teacher, asks. Only Charlotte Lee answers 'yes'. Charlotte was my main secret crush, but now she's Josh's squeeze. She sits across from me but it feels like a thousand miles. I've lusted after her for three years, but it took only a few days for Josh to turn my fantasies into his reality. She's small everywhere, even wears tiny round granny glasses, but my fantasies about her were huge.

Kirk Usher, the editor, starts talking, and talking, and talking, like he's afraid if sounds stop coming from his mouth, his vocal chords will dry up. If I believed in prayer, that miracle would be on my shortlist, along with rescuing Caitlin, nailing Charlotte and landing a job.

Kirk finally shuts up long enough for Mr. Jakes to speak. "How many of you are in the new creative writing club? How about you, Carson?" Mr. Jakes asks.

I try to hide my anger by looking away. For three years, I tried to get Mr. Jakes to start a creative writing class or at least a club, but he was always too busy. So we ended up with a sponsor — Dr. Stephanie Draper — a retired English professor who happens to be friends with Josh Brown's physician parents. At the first meeting, Josh was the only one she called by name.

"I heard Josh Brown was elected president," Mr. Jakes says.

I realize that no matter how good I am with words, I can't find one to describe the maelstrom of anger, happiness and frustration I feel about this club. Instead of creating stories, I should try to create words for all these mixed emotions that wreck my heart and rack my head. I'm feeling frushappanger.

"Josh is so hot," some freshman girl behind me says.

"But he's also cool," another girl adds, almost breathless.

I turn. "Maybe his porn name could be Luke Warm," I joke. They don't laugh.

"Jealous much?" the blonde one almost hisses. Truth is, I was jealous at the first meeting of the creative writing club. Josh presented something he wrote, while I sat in stone silence. I've dreamed so long of being a writer that I'm choking at the chance. Show off or shut up, I guess.

"Don't get your hopes up. Josh has a girlfriend already." I slap them down. I don't add that the girlfriend happens to be Charlotte. She'd been mine many times in my head and hand.

The girlfriend thing is so perplexing. I don't have a love life. I have a lust life. I can't figure how to move from the vertical world to the horizontal realm. My few so-called girlfriends have been interested more in the friend part than my interest in their girl parts. My exes are not just the opposite sex, they're opposed to sex with me. Unlike the girls on my screen, Thien was a prude mute. No matter how I touched her, which wasn't much, the only sound she made was to say "*No*". If I get another chance, I hope I'll think with my head, not just my horny.

"Banks, listen up," Kirk says. He's dressed to kill, which is good, since I want him dead.

"What is it, Kirk?" I overdramatically pronounce the 'k's in his name.

"Banks, your stories didn't suck, but only two? Normally what you lack in quality you make up for in quantity." Kirk laughs at his own words. He's his own — and only — best audience.

"Thanks for the input, Kirk," I say, which is Carson-speak for *Shut up, asshole.*

"The all-state story is good," Kirk says. It's killing him to compliment me. I'm getting the soft part of the palm. I'm flinching for the hard heel shot. "But my headline made it great."

"'All-State Ambition'," I say. "You're right, Kirk. Nobody wants to read about all-state athletes like Randall Martin or Gabrielle Gibson. It's all about your headline." I wrote a story about them last year, so Kirk wanted me to update their status. A running story, he calls it.

"I'm glad you see it my way," Kirk says, then leaves my sight like I flushed. I'd like to hate Kirk because he treats me like crap, but he is a good editor. I hate that fact even more.

I'm six days away from another chance to share my creative writing—my real writing, not fact regurgitation—and I've got nothing as good as what Josh shared. His story, called 'Reconsider Me' involved a smart, sensitive-type boy moving from best friend to boyfriend with a beautiful, mysterious girl. His story, according to Dr. Draper, *"yearned to answer the questions of the human heart"*.

Questions of the human heart? The pen clicks in my head as I rush to grab the yearbook from Caitlin's senior year, then grab an open computer. I open the yearbook page to 'Homecoming'. Caitlin's staring at the camera with a stoned expression, the same expression I saw so many times in our house, on her Facebook, in her vids, but not in those online photos I've found. With the yearbook in front of me, I click away on the keys. I'll change the names, but not the story, or at least what I know about Caitlin Autumn Banks'—or should I say Autumn's—fall.

Chapter Six

Excerpt from Autumn's Fall
'Homecoming Havoc'

"Are you drunk, little sister?" August asked his sister Autumn on homecoming night.

"No, I'm not, big brother," she replied. Her response would have been more believable if she hadn't staggered into the house or slurred her words. Her response — a lie and a denial — was all August heard anymore from his older sister. "I'm drunk and I'm high."

"You'll be in trouble," August said, sounding sad, angry and strangely protective.

"Listen, big brother! You got to know something!" Doesn't she realize she's shouting?

"What's that?" August asked, trying not to stare at his sister's outfit of stiletto ruby heels, tight, low, black jeans and a red Hollister top with a zipper farther south than north.

"Our parents are not going to kill me or give me away," she said, then laughed—a laugh that chilled August to his bones. "There's nothing they can do to me."

"But—" August started, but he couldn't argue with that logic—or lack thereof. He'd never been in trouble with his parents and neither had his older sister Amber. All the trouble in his house settled in the middle daughter, especially since the start of her senior year.

"You'll grow up, one day. You'll see," Autumn said, as she swayed from side to side. "You try to do good things, but they don't care. All I do is disappoint them, and myself."

August knew his fourteen-year-old words wouldn't make any difference. He'd listen from afar with a mixed grill of emotions as his parents handled Autumn's increasingly bad behavior. It seemed every night there was a fight, except for the nights when Autumn didn't come home. The fights were getting worse. The nights coming home late, or not at all, growing more frequent. August didn't understand anything but his helplessness. He wished he could do something and act heroic, like the characters he read about in fantasy fiction.

"Hey, Autumn, let's roll," called a male voice from the open door.

"I gotta get my things," Autumn said. "Dwayne, come in and entertain my big brother."

"You don't look so big." Dwayne, a classic biker, asked, "Why does she call you that?"

"I always wanted a young sister, while Autumn always wanted a big brother. We decided that since we couldn't change our places in the family, we'd change what we called each other," August said. The names stuck, even if their once-close relationship was now fractured.

August hated it when his oldest sister, Amber, called him 'baby brother', but nowhere as much as Autumn hated the phrase 'middle child' — or as much as he hated Dwayne. August didn't know Dwayne. He didn't want to know him. Like all her revolving door boyfriends, Dwayne had exited high school early. Autumn hung by a thin thread, which was a shame. Autumn was everything that August wanted to be — smart, popular and an attention magnet. Why couldn't she see it for herself? Except in her appearance, Autumn thought she was a failure compared to Amber.

"Dawg, your sister has a fine ass." Dwayne was white trash, but spoke Flint ghetto. He dressed in a black leather jacket, rode a silver Harley and had a big gold earring. He wasn't dressed for a high-school homecoming. He was dressed for pirating August's sister.

"I've got to go," August said, trying to flee fast.

"Wait up." Dwayne grabbed August by the belt and pulled him back, like some bully on the playground. Up close, Dwayne smelled like a brewery fire.

"Let me go," August said, but Dwayne held tightly then talked rapidly about nothing — nothing the keyword, as there was nothing August could do. He could feel his anger rise with the goosebumps on his arms. Seconds after the furnace clicked on, Dwayne shouted, "Is that a rat?"

August ignored him as he watched Mr. Innocent race through the room. The dog, a Boston terrier pug mix that August's mom found through a rescue group in Texas, had been a gift for his tenth birthday. The dog had yet to grow hair for the cold Michigan climate. The minute the furnace clicked on, he would race toward the heat vent in August's room.

Dwayne finally let go. August started to leave but stopped when Autumn emerged from her room. Her low-cut gold homecoming meshed with her long blonde hair. The dress their dad had insisted she return, which meant she wouldn't. But the dress wasn't all that was gold. Necklaces, rings and bracelets. Autumn didn't work other than helping their sick grandmother, but that was unpaid. He knew their parents had ended her allowance as one of their punishments. August assumed that Dwayne was Autumn's alchemist.

"Damn, you are so hot," Dwayne said then handed something to Autumn.

"Are you still going to homecoming?" August asked his sister. It took her a second to respond, she was too busy lighting up the cigarette Dwayne had passed her.

"You're keeping track of me now too, big brother?" she said, then laughed. She blew the smoke in the air. August thought the smoke served as a perfect metaphor as August watched his sister's life burn down.

"Mom and Dad wanted to take pictures," August said, looking nervously at the clock. They were never late for anything, so August figured they were just avoiding another scene.

"So they can compare them with the Princess Amber," Autumn shot back. "I'm sure her homecoming was perfect, like everything else she does, while I can't do anything right."

August didn't say anything, just like he'd never heard his parents say anything of the sort. He didn't know everything his parents thought or said, but he knew this competition between Amber and Autumn existed only in one place—Autumn's increasingly distorted brain.

"Take this picture!" Autumn thrust a middle finger toward the stairway at a family photo from an Easter morning years ago. Everyone in those pictures was smiling, especially August whenever he stood next to Autumn.

"Why are you acting this way?" August asked, unable to understand yet wanting to know so he could change her. August loved his sister so much, but hated who she was becoming.

"When I'm rich and famous, everybody will take pictures of me," she said with a smirk.

August didn't respond. He didn't tell his sister that he'd seen her Facebook page. Back in her freshman year, the pictures had been like those of any other girl, but everything had changed that summer. Cancer attacked Grandma, change invaded Autumn. August had watched helplessly as the Autumn, who babysat him for years, helped him with his homework and did everything a big sister was supposed to do, slowly disappeared while this new creature emerged, obsessed with herself and fame. The bad behavior, August guessed, wasn't her acting out like a child, but lashing out like an adult frustrated that they are unable to achieve their dreams. What would it take to make her happy?

"They'll be angry," August finally said.

"Good," Autumn said, then laughed. The laughter was drowned out by the clicking of her high heels across the kitchen floor. August looked out of the window. There was no limo, just Dwayne's chrome horse. August realized that it wouldn't be long before Autumn walked out of the door and never came back.

What kept him awake was deciding if Autumn leaving home forever would be a dream fulfilled or a nightmare descended. August thought that maybe his family's dreams and nightmares were the same, and they all resided in Autumn. Autumn controlled all their lives and Autumn's life was spinning out of control.

Chapter Seven

Thursday, October 21st
Creative writing club meeting

"Any comments on 'Homecoming Havoc'?" Dr. Draper asks after she finishes reading my story, but nobody knows I wrote it. She's using something called a 'blind read'. I don't blink or twitch.

She glances at the wall of silence. None of these people knew Caitlin, and none know me well enough to realize this is anything but fiction. I changed her name to Autumn, probably like she's changed her name to some nasty porn name.

"Anyone?" Dr. Draper asks. Her idea for the 'blind read' was that nobody would feel embarrassed to talk for fear of offending a friend if they didn't know who wrote the piece. Only a few of us handed in anything, and just one person volunteered to skip the blind reading and share his work aloud. Josh Brown. His reading was supposed to last five minutes. He used fifteen. When Josh started to read, it was as if the party host had entered the room as every eye turned to him.

His new story, 'Searching for a Heart', was about a smart, sensitive-type boy falling in love with a beautiful, mysterious girl. The boy's obsessed with first lines of novels and uses them in conversation. His story was a green light for compliments, but the color changed to red as Dr. Draper asked for comments about 'Homecoming Havoc'. If a story falls in the woods and no one—

Finally, Kirk speaks up to comment on my story. That doesn't surprise, but does worry me. He thinks he's smarter than everyone else and always has to be first with his normally negative opinion. Once again, he's true to form, saying about my story that, "The writing needs sharpening. It's too heavy-handed."

As Kirk's speaking, I notice how he's looking around the room, trying to catch the eye of the writer he's trashing, but I'm stone facing it. Some bullies need to see the terror. Instead, I'm yawning. Next to comment is Candy Tanner with her monotone voice. I can't see past her fake blondeness and real blandness. She's dull and her web comics she brags about all the time are just dreadful. "I wouldn't say heavy-handed, more like ham-fisted," she cuts.

I pretend to listen as Dr. Draper reads the next piece, but I'm not that strong. I collapse into myself and try staring at my black Chucks to avoid Josh's emerald eyes, but I can't look away. Josh is holding Charlotte's hand with one hand, the other strokes his soul patch as if he was deep in thought. With his hipster-thin glasses, and dark green clothes—because black would be too cliché—he looks like Johnny Depp, the dream lover of emo, Goth and nerd-proud girls. Looking around, most girls in this club fall into those groups. All the poems Dr. Draper read were about roses, razor blades and romantic vampires. These girls all loved Josh's story, using words like *'charming'* and *'delightful'*. He's got his clique — or harem — in his corner.

The only girl who didn't say anything about Josh's story was Gabrielle Gibson. It's odd she's here. I'd pegged her as a ball-bouncing blockhead, not a writer. She wears white Chucks, a Detroit Shock T-shirt and an uncomfortable expression. She's out of place in this club, but that's normal for her at FHS. There are not many six-foot-tall black girls in the 'burbs and none in this club.

Dr. Draper reminds us of the next meeting and encourages us to keep writing. Despite the negative reaction, I'm going to stay with this story. Maybe if I write about Caitlin's past, I'll find clues to locate her in the present. Since I don't have access to a time machine, I can't change her history, but I need to better understand it.

I'm starting to exit when I feel a tap on my shoulder. I turn to see Gabrielle.

"Carson, do you remember me?" she asks in a tiny voice for someone so tall.

"Sure," I lie. This is the second time I've ever spoken to her that I recall. I interviewed her last year for that story, but I didn't bother this year. Caitlin's body work is making me brain damaged.

"Do you remember what you wrote about me last year?" she says, a little bit louder.

"Right, about you maybe being all-state in three sports. Did you like it?"

"You called me The Great Gabby." She's looking at the floor, not me.

"You're a great athlete," I lie. I never saw her play since I don't do girls' sports. It just sounded like a cool nickname. By reputation, though, she's one of the best female athletes in school. "I was trying to impress readers of the sports page and fellow F. Scott Fitzgerald fans."

"Well, I think you're a great writer," she says. "I liked your story."

"Randall said so, too." Unlike Caitlin, who lived for compliments, they embarrass me.

"Not the story in the paper about me," she says, but I respond with a blank stare at her interest. "The one about the girl Autumn that Dr. Draper just read. You wrote that, didn't you?"

"Maybe," I mumble, as I stare down at her Chucks. Her feet are almost as big as mine.

"They were wrong. It was a good story," she says. "But I hope it has a happy ending."

I pause, but then say, "That's out of a writer's control. It's where the story goes."

"Make sure Autumn gets a second chance."

I look up and she's staring at me, hard.

"But Great Gabby, Fitzgerald said there are no second acts in American lives."

"Then maybe Mr. F. Scott Fitzgerald was wrong," she says with a dark scowl that melts quickly into the brightest smile. "Carson, doesn't everybody deserve a second chance?"

Chapter Eight

Friday, October 22nd

"Hey, Tim, what do you know about Gabrielle Gibson?" I ask, as cool as the glass of iced water that Tim sets in front of me at First Wok during the non-dinner rush. I'm cutting down on caffeine so I can maybe sleep rather than staying up all night surfing for clues about Caitlin.

"Who?" Mr. Owl replies, which is about the answer I'd expect from him. The divide between ball bouncers and test takers at Fenton is Grand Canyon size.

"Never mind." I shrug it off, but really it's 'always mind' because I notice I can't stop thinking about Gabby. As I look for more pictures of Caitlin and a way to contact her, I find myself lingering on photos of tall black girls rather than busty blondes. I find myself at school looking for Gabby—we don't have any classes together—and she's easy to spot. Within her peer group—all athletes, most of them black—it's easy to tell

Clicked

from how they gather around that she's the alpha female. Unlike me, who gets attention with my smart mouth, she's got a physical presence.

"You going to the football game?" Tim asks. I know he cares nothing about football, but he cares about me, so he asks. He's got the friend thing down to a science.

"Only way I can get published!" I shout in mock excitement. Tim doesn't laugh because maybe he hears the angry undercurrent in my sarcastic tone. I think about the perfect prose of Josh's 'Searching for a Heart' story compared to anything I've ever written and realize I should feel lucky that Mr. Jakes allows my vapid verbiage even in the crappy school paper.

Tim heads toward the front to greet some customers. I open my notebook, click my pen but nothing comes to mind—no image, no metaphor, nothing but a blank page mocking me.

I turn away from the white page and see the black glasses and long black hair. Longer legs and tiny breasts, neither pair she'd let my face get between. Thien. With her family. I consider putting the glass of water against my face to cool the burning blush of shame streaking across it. Thanks to Thien, I wear two scarlet letters, except the AA stands for aggressive asshole.

Thien, two little brothers and her parents walk toward me. Even if they weren't standing and I wasn't sitting, I'd bet they'd still be looking down at me, not that I don't deserve it.

"Carson," Thien says. These are the first words she's said to me since 'Take me home, now' after my post-prom fiasco. I hope she's not said anything about what happened to anyone, in particular her parents. They thought I was nice. They thought I was a gentleman.

45

Wrong. Wrong. If her dad doesn't punch me, then I'll know my secret's safe, and I'm still sorry.

"Hey." I don't say her name, even if I used to utter her name when fantasizing about her in the shower. She says nothing in words, but readjusts the black-framed glasses on her pinched-in-disgust face, as if reminding me of my dirty deed. I wait until she passes by until I breathe again.

I try to write but everything comes out wrong. I can't get the images in my mind to come out on the page. I think all the best writing ends up trapped in my elbow. If I could just crack it open, maybe I'd produce something as good as Josh. *If* is the heaviest word in the dictionary.

Who am I kidding? While I've been here in Fenton writing about sports in barely literate English and taking college prep but not AP classes, Josh's been off at some private school where everybody probably speaks French, goes to the Riviera for vacation and writes flawless fiction to start each day. He's highbrow. I'm not even lowbrow. Compared to Josh, I'm unibrow.

My eyes dart back and forth between the blank page and the blank slate I wish I had with Thien. Life doesn't have a 'clear history' like Chrome, nor can you go through life incognito. Just like in the virtual world, you leave a trail everywhere you go, but if so, why can't I find Caitlin's virtual vapor? How can a person disappear for years or stay hidden even while naked?

"Hey, Carson, can I ask you something?" Tim sits down at the table. Even though he's not working hard—there are only four other tables besides Thien's family's—he's sweating.

I think of a smart-ass response since that's my brand, but seeing Thien deflates the humor balloon that keeps me afloat. I nod, close the notebook and cup my ear with my right hand.

"You going to Charlotte's Halloween party?" Tim asks.

Charlotte. Before Thien, before anyone else, there was Charlotte. "I don't think so." Wanting her and getting nowhere all those years hurt. Knowing she's with Josh kills me dead. "Doubt it."

"Carson, let's go." The favor balance is way out of proportion between us. I owe him.

"I hate Halloween." I wonder if Tim remembers why. No look of sorrow or sympathy washes over his face. We weren't friends then, so maybe I never told him. Kept him innocent about parts of my life just like I've yet to tell him about Caitlin. Tim does so much for me, so this is the least I can do for him — separate my dirty life from his clean one.

"I take almost all AP classes, so you know how few girls other than Charlotte I see on a given day?" Tim asks. "She plays tennis, so I bet those girls from her team will be there along with people in your newspaper class and your writing club. What else do you have to do?"

"Thanks for that!" I yell way too loud. He laughs, so that's something. "But if Charlotte is there, that means Josh is there. I'll wear shades so I'm not blinded by his brilliance."

Tim starts to talk, but spinning spokes click in my head. Charlotte. Tennis. Gabby. Tim must notice that the perma-frown I'd worn since Thien walked in the door surrenders to a smile.

"So, you're in, Carson?"

Images of Thien, Charlotte and Gabby spill like a page of porn thumbnails across my mind. In? Yes, I want to be in something, someone, somehow, someway. "I'll even drive."

Another customer walks in, causing Tim to exit the table, leaving me alone with my thoughts, which give way to fantasy. Connecting the two is the hardest task on earth. The women on my computer screen and girls in my daily grind are light years away from my reality. Maybe that can be Tim's first project at MIT, to build a machine to bridge the great divide of despair.

Chapter Nine

Sunday, October 31st
Halloween

"Where are you going?" Mom asks. There's always an edge of her assuming the worst.

"Some of the creative writing club people are getting together," I remind her. She doesn't press me if 'get-together' is just another name for party. It is, but for me the word party is a noun, not a verb.

"You're feeling better?" she asks. I launch into a fake coughing fit. I spent most of yesterday looking for Caitlin. I found more photos, but still no way to find her. I sent out more emails to companies, but no one ever responds. Writing to porn companies in Chatsworth, CA, is like a child writing to Santa at the North Pole—the mail goes out, but it never comes back.

"Just tired," I say.

"I'm sorry you haven't found work. Maybe next month," she says, trying to sound upbeat.

I zip up my gray hoodie then head out to Mom's Malibu. In the good days, Mom and Dad got a new GM car every year, but the good days are gone. The Malibu stays until it falls apart. It survived many Caitlin-caused accidents. Our family flows so nicely — Carol was an accident, Caitlin caused accidents and I'm accident-prone, although I've yet to bend the fender.

Before I pick up Tim to join me at the party, I drive around the neighborhood where lawns fill with 'For sale' signs like weeds. I think I should tell my parents about Caitlin, but can't imagine how. Do I say, *Mom, Dad, I've got some good news and bad news. The good news is Caitlin's alive, the bad news is she's fucking men for both money and show. Good times.*

I bury my dark thoughts and pick up Tim at First Wok. He looks glum when he climbs in.

"Sorry. I asked my uncle. He can't hire you," Tim says as he sits down. He's slurping from an oversized cup of Mountain Dew, the drug of choice of straight edge Honor Society types.

"It's okay," I grumble. "It's not like I have anyone to spend money on anyway."

"I resemble that remark," Tim cracks, although he's not laughing.

"You don't need a girlfriend. You need a secretary," I say. "You're too busy."

"Just because I'm a math and science AP class taking, NHS participating, hard-working and obedient son, doesn't mean that I'm not interested in getting laid," Tim says. "But alas..."

"I know a lass who would be perfect for you!"

"Who's that?"

"Thien Nguyen," I say. "It would be beauty and brains, but no breasts." Despite my lust of big-boobed porn blondes, in real life, I favor girls with tiny tits like Thien and Charlotte.

"Dude, I don't think so," he says, oblivious to my conflicted enthusiasm.

I want my best friend to get a girlfriend. That's a guy thing. I want my ex, Thien, to be happy. That's a guilt thing.

"Well, tonight I'm taking a chance," I say. "The first drunk girl I see, I'm hitting on."

"I don't think it's that kind of party," Tim says, then opens up the brown paper bag he brought with him. "Alrrrrrrrrrrrrrrrrrrrrrrrrrrright!"

Tim pulls out and puts on a black eye patch. He dons a pirate hat and tosses the bag into the back seat filled with Mom's 'For sale' yard signs. I've never seen a 'Sold' one in the car.

I try not to laugh too loud as I ask, "Where's the rest of the costume?"

"This is enough," he says, trying to act serious. As serious as an eighteen-year-old overweight Chinese guy wearing an eye patch and oversize *Star Wars* shirt while drinking an ocean full of Mountain Dew can be. We drive to Charlotte's party she's holding at her parents' lakefront McMansion. Josh junkies and Charlotte's friends—newspaper nerds, writing clubbers and tennis types—should fill the place. They've got many major cliques covered, but entering the house is more like walking into the costume room in the theater department. Everybody's dressed up but me.

To no surprise, the most dressed up is Josh. Unlike Tim with his stupid eye patch and stupider hat, Josh is a full-blown pirate and his merry mates are gathered around him. Charlotte's decked out in a similar costume and attached to his right hip like the fake sword is to his left. I scan the crowd for guys I know and girls I want to know, which is every girl in school except Thien and Charlotte. She's taken and Thien's not talking to me, for good reason. Tim heads off for food, while I move away from the glorious glow of Josh, the Sun God Pirate.

"Welcome to the no-costume club," I hear a girl's voice say. I turn around and there's Gabrielle Gibson standing behind me. Like me, she's dressed normally. We both sport gray hoodies, blue jeans, Chucks and white T-shirts, like identical twins, except for gender, skin color and hairstyle. My hair's styled, hers natural.

"Why bother?" I say with a shrug.

"Just be yourself, right?"

"Even if I dressed up for Halloween, no way I'd impress anyone in this crowd."

"So, if you can't win, then you don't play?" she asks. A bemused expression coupled with a shrug serves as my reply. "You miss one hundred percent of the shots you don't take."

"Wayne Gretzky said that," I say. "Sorry. I'm loaded with useless sports trivia."

She takes a step closer, then asks, "Have you worked any more on Autumn's story?"

"Why do you think I wrote it?" I whisper. I'm trying not to smile, but failing badly.

"Because it was the best story."

"Except for Josh's perfect prose."

"I guess." She shrugs. She seems unimpressed by Josh and his assembly of acolytes, while I'm both appalled and envious. She kicks the floor with her right foot, which seems to set off a mischievous look on her face. "I bet Josh didn't drive here from school."

"Why do you say that?" I ask.

"I assume he just walked across the lake," she says, but unlike me, she doesn't hide the big smile on her face—a face I've never looked at before. Just like she's a little taller than most girls, Gabrielle's face... Well, her features seem larger, in particular big brown eyes that squint when a smile breaks out over her less than perfect light brown skin. "Sorry. That was mean."

"You miss one hundred percent of the insults you don't deliver."

She laughs, then that smile follows. She's too smart, pretty, funny and impressive to be available. She must be a lez.

"I just saw him and Charlotte head off. Everybody is pairing up. Who you here with?"

"Tim Wang. The Chinese Pirate. No beard. Johnny Dweeb. Wrong John Silver."

She laughs. "I shouldn't have laughed. That was wrong. Funny, but wrong," she adds.

"I think you just wrote my epitaph."

"Epi-what?" she asks.

"That's the saying they put on your grave," I tell her.

"Mine's going to say Gabrielle Gibson, three-sport Olympic Gold Medalist."

"If you win three gold medals, then everyone will call you The Great Gabby."

"Maybe you can be my press agent?" she asks.

I fake a cough to kill time. Is she flirting with me? She must be, because the response from deep in my brain and between my legs wants to be *I'd love to press against you*. I've talked with Gabby twice before, but it's like the horny switch just clicked up to ten.

"Carson, don't you wanna be my agent?" she asks, breaking the silence. Before I can answer, she looks away from me, staring now at the floor. "Don't bother. I suck."

"Don't say that. You're great."

"If I'm so great, then why did our volleyball team lose yesterday? Because I suck."

"Well, volleyball is a team sport. It's not your fault. What's that line coaches always use? There's no 'I' in the word team?" I remind her.

"Yes, but there is an 'I' in the word win," she says. Now, it's my turn to laugh.

"Who are you here with?" A minute ago I wouldn't have cared, but now, it matters.

"My friends don't really go to parties like this."

"Why not?"

"Well, do you see anybody else here who looks like me?"

"Point, Gabrielle Gibson," I say, trying to sound like a TV tennis announcer, but she gives me a fake dirty look, complete with hands on hips. "Um, I mean, point goes to The Great Gabby."

"I should be studying for the SATs."

"I took the SAT," I say. "Do you know what the perfect score is on the SAT?"

She shrugs her strong shoulders.

"Twenty-four hundred," I tell her. "Now, ask me what I got on my SAT?"

"Okay, Carson, what did you score on your SAT?"

"Twenty-four hundred!"

She mouths the word 'wow', then I say, "Four hundred the first time, eight hundred the second time and twelve hundred the third time."

She laughs and that wide, gorgeous smile lights up her face.

"Shouldn't you be at home studying then, to obtain such greatness?" I ask.

"Shouldn't you be writing about Autumn?" Gabby counters.

"How did you know that I wrote — not that I'm admitting anything — the Autumn story?"

"When people talked about that story, you were wearing your game face," she says.

"Man, you're good," I say. "You can spike, shoot and serve. What can't you do?"

"Party," she says as she holds up a can of Diet Coke. "I bet you don't either, do you?"

I nod, but I should have been shaking my amazed head. How does this girl know me so well?

"Because of Autumn, right? In the story you wrote how she partied, so you avoid it."

"Autumn's just somebody in a story," I lie. "She's not real."

"She's real to me." Gabrielle takes a sip of Coke, but I feel a gulp in my throat.

"Maybe, I don't know," I mumble. I can dream about girls, but I *so* can't talk to them.

"Remember, the story needs a happy ending." Her smile vanishes. There's a darkness at the edges of her eyes. She curls her big left hand into a fist. "We all need happy endings."

"I promise," I say as she moves closer. "What's wrong, Gabrielle?"

"Don't you mean The Great Gabby?" she whispers. "I just hate feeling like a loser."

Before I can say anything else, she walks away. Since Josh has made me feel like a loser, I know how that feeling destroys a person and distorts your judgment. She throws the pop can in the trash and heads outside.

I follow her outside and down into the big back yard. A cool fall wind blows out here. Inside Josh's light warms everyone. Something's got to change. Now.

"Gabby, you're not a loser." I put my hands gently on those strong shoulders. I take a deep breath, then serve the ball across the net. "What can I do to make you believe that?"

She uncurls her fist, opens her hand and puts it on the back of my neck, pulling my face next to hers as she returns the volley. "You could kiss me."

As our lips come together, I swear I hear a click, because the kiss is not too soft, not too hard. It's just right.

Chapter Ten

Monday, November 1st

"What happened to you last night?" Tim asks. I ignore him because I'm too busy staring at Gabby. She's across the cafeteria, sitting with her volleyball teammates. I'm with Tim, as usual, and his NHS buds.

"Did Carson tell you guys what he dressed up as for Halloween?" Tim asks the table. I give him a strange look, but before anyone can answer, he chimes in, "The Invisible Man. He drags me to a party. One minute he's there and the next minute he's gone. Vanishing act."

"Kind of like his sister," Kevin Baker says. Kevin's one of my few old buds from junior high who I still see on occasion who knew Caitlin. He also had the biggest crush on her. I shoot Kevin a burning glare that would make Cyclops from the X-Men envious.

"Tim, I got busy," I say. I take a bite of my burger rather than a bite out of Kevin's face. Tim looks apologetic for saying something. He never asked where

I went, so I didn't need to lie. Tim's many things. One is honest to a fault. Like his study habits, that doesn't rub off on me either.

"Busy like a bee," Kevin cracks.

"I best be going," I say.

"You be talking like you be a playa, sucka!" Kevin points toward Gabby and her friends. There are maybe twenty African American girls at school. Many of them, like Gabby, moved to Fenton from Flint, and most do play or star in sports. "You should roll with them nappy—"

"Knock it off," I snap, and everybody looks surprised. At school, I'm a get along, go along guy. I just want to write stories, crack jokes and stay off people's shitlists.

"What's your deal?" Kevin snaps back. "I'm just kidding around, Carson."

"Never mind," I say as I walk away from the table. Last night, the last thing before the last kiss, Gabby told me that if we started something, we'd need to keep it secret. I didn't ask why, but with racist friends like Kevin, I can't say that's not a bad idea.

As I navigate the noise of the hallway, the clatter sounds like life's ugly twin sister—irony—laughing at me. I finally maybe find a girlfriend, but I can't tell anyone. I finally get a chance to share my writing, only to learn that it's not that good. I finally get these chances to succeed, but all I do is fear failure. The ringing of the class bell as I walk into Mr. Jake's room whiplashes me into the present and the problem at hand—finding a way to spend time with Gabby without anyone finding out. The answer's as obvious as the sour look on Kirk's face as he sits at his imperial editor's desk.

"Can I trade assignments?" I ask Kirk at the start of class. I hate asking for favors.

"Depends," he says. Kirk loves his little power trips.

"I'm tired of covering boys' sports," I lie as the last part of my sentence gets overwhelmed by his loud sighing. "I want to cover girls' sports, like volleyball."

"Let me think about it," Kirk responds.

"I'm going to cover their game Thursday," I say firmly. He doesn't know how much I resent him, but not because he's the editor. I never wanted that job—too much drama, too little writing. No, it's because of his comments on my story. I think Kirk Usher is Greek for 'asshole critic'.

"Let me think about it," he says, adding another sigh for emphasis.

"I'll write you a story right away," I say. "I bet the team is practicing after school."

I start to walk away, when Kirk says, "Hey, what did you think of Josh's story in creative writing club?" Josh's story was the only one that Kirk didn't criticize.

"It was okay," I admit.

"You should see his column for the next paper. It's fabulous," Kirk says.

"I anticipate greatly reading each impeccable sentence." I double-dip each syllable in sarcasm.

"You don't have to," Kirk says, then hands me a sheet of paper. I scan it over. The column is a conversation between Josh and his imaginary evil twin sister. I try not to laugh, but it's funny, so that's hard not to do. I try not to cry because it is so good. That's harder yet. I try not to hate Josh, but that's too easy. Instead of handing the paper back to Kirk, I let it fall.

"Sorry. You'd think I could hold a light piece of paper with my heavy hands," I say.

His words about my story don't register, yet somehow it feels like another small victory in this unexpected winning streak.

* * * *

"Gabrielle, one second," I say as she walks toward the girls' locker room. After school, I'd run as fast as I could—which isn't very fast, or graceful—to try to catch her before she started practice. On the way over, I thought I'd practice what I would say to her, but for all my creative skills, I couldn't think of anything to say, so instead I ask, "Can I talk with you?"

"Carson, I can't," she says, then disappears into the locker room. Can't what? Can't talk to me now? Can't talk to me ever? Can't see me? Why does 'can't' seem to be the most popular word in the dictionary when people are talking to me about something that matters?

I stand by the locker room for a few minutes, then decide I can't take no for an answer. Pulling out a notebook from my backpack, I walk into the gym and spy the volleyball coach, Ms. Gleason, sitting in her office. A couple of lies later, she agrees to let me watch practice.

As I watch Gabrielle—The Great Gabby—dominate the game, I realize she is to the other girls on the court what Josh is to creative writing. If I hate Josh for being so talented, do these other girls feel the same about Gabby? That's why Caitlin had so few real female friends. She saw them as rivals and resented any success. The almost perfect person is the home of the rage.

As I watch the ball go back and forth across the net, I wonder what happened. Gabby served, I returned, but now she won't—or is it can't—serve again. Only when practice is over does Gabby look at me. She waits until everyone leaves the court, waves then blows me a kiss. Like one of her serves, the airborne kiss is powerful, perfect and makes an impact. Poets write how love is like oxygen, but I don't need to be a chemistry king like Tim to know that's wrong. Love is helium, and I'm floating like a balloon into a bright blue sky.

Chapter Eleven

Thursday, November 4th

"Carson, how did I do?" Gabby whispers as we drive through a perfect fall night.

"You were great," I tell her, unsure why she needs me to tell her things she already knows. As always, she wears a baggy sports T-shirt, this time the Tigers, while I'm dressed up, for me, with a button-down oxford. Liking someone makes you like yourself.

She sits close to me. It feels right. "No, I missed some spikes, blew some serves."

"Gabby, you won the tournament," I remind her.

She laughs. "I know, but it's sad, though. My last high-school volleyball game — ever."

"Well, if you serve up a kiss, I'd be happy to return it."

"Maybe, or maybe I'll spike your skinny ass!" she jokes.

"Ouch! Rejected!" I feign injury.

"No, timeout," she says, then kisses me. It's the first time we've been alone since the party. She's busy serving and spiking balls across the net. I'm busy still surfing the Net for Caitlin. At school, Gabby's ignored me like she said she would, but online she's responded. She didn't explain those actions and I didn't ask. What matters isn't the past but her presence next to me. In person, I'm responding as only a seventeen-year-old guy who's so horny he can barely see. "Pull over."

I can't tell her that while I'm used to driving and punning with Tim, trying to keep it funny, keeping my hand on her shoulder and one hand on the wheel is making me very nervous. I'm a good driver, but it's mainly because I'm a terrified driver. "Anyplace special?" I ask.

"Did you and Thien have someplace special?" she says, sounding angry.

"Wow, foul, foul, foul," I say, then whistle.

"Okay, that was reaching in." She puts my arm back around her shoulders. "Anyplace but the school parking lot or All Star Towing off Owen Road is fine."

"Wow, how sad, that towing place sounds sooooooooooo romantic!"

She laughs. "Well, actually, my dad owns it."

"Really?"

"He owns, operates and seems to work there twenty-four hours a day."

"That's so cool," I say. "He works for himself, not some big company like my dad did."

"Dad always says you can't live the American dream sleeping in somebody else's bed."

"He sounds like a great guy. I can't wait to—"

"Pull over, please, Carson. We need to talk about that."

"Okay." I pull Mom's Malibu into the parking lot of a Mobil gas station. Since I've yet to betray them, I don't think my folks check the mileage on the car, a trick they used with Caitlin. She countered by crashing Mom's car, then using increasingly older and scarier-looking guys like Dwayne as chauffeurs. "How's this? It looks like they have their own tow trucks."

Gabby nods in agreement. I respond by moving my face closer. She smells fresh from the shower. No makeup or jewelry, Gabby's all natural, even her hair.

"Wait, just a second," she says. "A couple of rules if this is going to work."

"This?" I ask, arching an eyebrow.

"This," she responds, and we share our longest, best kiss of the evening and ever.

"Nobody can know, especially my dad," she reminds me. "And we can't go to school dances, hold hands in the hall or any of that stupid high-school couples stuff."

"Are you ashamed of me?" I ask, half joking, half terrified.

"No, not at all," she says. "And I know what you're thinking."

I just smile because she has no idea what I'm thinking. If she could read my mind, we'd be in the back seat engaged in activities with our mouths other than talking.

"It's not because you're white and I'm black," she says firmly. "That's not it at all."

"Really?" I doubt her only because everything in the Flint area is still about white and black.

She kisses me again. "It's just complicated. Just trust me, okay?"

"Okay." I realize that at this point I'd say anything to be with Gabby, somebody that I barely knew existed a few weeks ago.

"I have to be able to trust you." As she repeats that word 'trust' again, she doesn't sound like a three sport all-star. She sounds like she could break with just a push. "Promise you will never lie to me or break that trust."

"Promise it," I say, sealing the deal with another kiss as my hands start to explore her.

"You wanna play on my court, you gotta follow my rules," she says, moving my hand away. I nod in agreement, then she says, "I'd better get home. We can chat later tonight."

"Um, that might be a problem," I explain. "I'm trying not to be online so much."

Just moments after promising she can trust me, I have to lie to her. I sometimes wish that Caitlin had lied more to my parents to protect them from the truth. I keep fibbing to myself that I'll stay offline because the temptation is too great, and Caitlin is no closer. "I'm just busy with school, college stuff, the paper and writing, I don't have time to chat, but for you, I will—"

"Do nothing differently. You've made a decision. I know how hard it is to make a tough decision, and it's harder to stick to it." She runs her hands over my arms, which are nowhere as muscular as hers are. "I think it will be a lot more interesting to see you in person."

"Interesting?" I say, then arch an eyebrow, but she's in a very serious place, I can tell.

I move to kiss her again, but she turns away. "Carson, just hold me. That's all I need."

"That's not too complicated, but can I ask you one thing?"

She nods.

"How have you kept your other boyfriends secret, including from everybody at school?"

"I haven't had any other boyfriends at Fenton," she answers.

"Ah, saving the best for last!"

"Carson, I've been really lonely most of my time at Fenton. I mean, sports fill my time and my friends fill my life, but you know, it's not the same."

I think about Tim, my few other friends, my writing, and pull her a little closer.

"Most of the male athletes, I think, are a little scared of me. I'm sorry if this sounds so conceited, but I'm better at my sports than most of them are at theirs," she says. "And other guys don't find girl athletes interesting or attractive, so I've poured all my energy into excelling." I don't point out that most other guys are idiots, but I suspect she knows.

"Me too. I put all my energy into writing, but why bother with Lord Josh on the scene?"

Gabby laughs. "Just because you strive to be the best, Carson, doesn't mean you always will be. I don't make every shot, win every game, but I always work hard. I don't quit."

"It just seems —" I start, but stop my whining. "You're right, Gabby. I mean, Great Gabby."

"And, Carson, you're something else," Gabby says as I push the car into Drive. As she leans in against me, I know she's wrong. I'm not something else, I'm *part* of something else. Something secret. Something complicated. Something good.

* * * *

When I get home, Mom's in bed, but Dad's still up. He's watching the Red Wings but wearing a blue and silver Lions T-shirt. He sips the one beer he allows himself each evening. I'm sure his sponsor wouldn't approve, but the addictive gene fits tight in the Banks family.

"How was the game?" he yells over the TV. Dad never mutes the TV. He got so used to raising his voice with Caitlin that he's just used to shouting as normal volume.

"We won," I say, then try to start upstairs. "I need to write it up for the paper."

"Why the sudden interest in girls' sports?"

For the second time in about twenty minutes, I lie to protect myself and my dad from the truth. It's not only that Dad wouldn't approve of Gabby, but he can never meet her, especially if he reverts to his heavy drinking daze. When Dad was TUI—talking under the influence—he'd rave on and stories about how 'they' ruined Flint would fall like bombs from a drone. "I was bored with boys' sports. I needed a change."

"Okay," he says, sounding not skeptical at all. Since he doesn't expect me to lie to him, especially about something so trivial, he lets it pass.

"I gotta go," I say, then once again start toward the stairs.

"Watch some hockey with your old man." He waves me over, and I comply out of guilt.

As we're watching the game, we fall back into easy patter about the action on the ice. Even as we're talking, however, I think how Caitlin resented the time Dad and I spent together. She'd scream that I was Dad's favorite while Carol was Mom's. All the screaming and acting out became a self-fulfilling prophesy. Just as it was

Caitlin's time with Carol off to college, Grandma got sick, causing Mom to spend time with her rather than Caitlin. Mom put up with Caitlin's complaining until her senior year, when they tried getting tough. Since Caitlin wouldn't work — wouldn't even look except for modeling jobs, which were sorely lacking in Fenton — they made her take care of our sick grandma.

At first Caitlin resisted, but everybody was surprised by how much Caitlin seemed to enjoy helping out since none of us had ever known her to do anything that wasn't about her. It wasn't until Thanksgiving that I learned why Caitlin spent so much time with Grandma. For a while, I was the only one that knew. It was something secret. Something complicated. Something unforgiveable — and something worth writing about in the next chapter of Autumn's story.

Chapter Twelve

Friday, November 5th

"Big day tomorrow, right?" Dad asks as I walk through the back door into the kitchen. I wonder if he can tell from my almost bruised but smiling lips that I'm studying Gabby more than I'm studying my test-prep guides. Tim's due over in a bit so I can stop lying and start learning.

"ACT," I say.

"You deserve this. I know you're juggling a lot with school, the newspaper and now this test." Dad hands me a cold bottle of Miller High Life. It's like a TV commercial, I feel like I'm in a dream. It's great to see Dad sticking to one nightly beer. The only good thing about Caitlin leaving is Dad's drinking discipline.

"Thanks, Dad." He motions me to follow him to the kitchen table. Once we're seated, he offers up his bottle to me. The glass bottles click together and the beer tastes great.

"I talked to Carol today," he says. "She's not coming home for the holidays."

"Why not?" Normally I would've known that from Facebook. Carol updates her Facebook more often than Lil Wayne drops the f-bomb. Her status should say 'Carol is changing her status again'. But to avoid porn, I've been offline for two days and out of touch.

"The economy's still bad in some places, not just here in Michigan," Dad says.

I let the silence chill the beer and the conversation, then ask, "Are we going to lose the house?" I'd overheard how they'd done a second mortgage to help pay for Carol's college.

He stalls with a long sip, then smiles. "Not if your mom can sell it first." He laughs, but there's a dark tone that undercuts the light joke. When Caitlin left, she took part of Mom and Dad with her. They don't fight as much as they did when Caitlin was here, mainly because they don't talk as much. It's hard to fight with someone when you're rarely in the same room and don't sleep in the same bed. Their marriage was collateral damage from Caitlin's path of destruction.

"What about college?" With the ACTs tomorrow, college is on my mind. Not as much as it should be, or as much as Caitlin, or Gabby, but it's there nonetheless.

"Son, just trust us. It's going to work out," he says, trying to sound confident. Sadly, it's the same tone I heard in his voice about GM rehiring experienced workers and about Caitlin coming home that first year after she ran away. My dad lacks credibility as a fortune teller. His promises are not really lies. They're just unanswered prayers.

"Thanks for the beer," I say, then finish it. The micro-buzz from the beer makes me think about Caitlin. It would be so easy to blame everything that happened on drugs, alcohol or bad influences. And I was the worst of them all in some ways. I was a wreck my freshman year, making new friends, losing old ones and hating myself. Caitlin whined about how my parents didn't have time for her because they were dealing with what she called my 'immature shit'.

"Good luck on your test tomorrow," Dad says

"Tim's coming over to study for a bit. Is that okay?"

Dad nods. But he looks like he wants me to stay, wants to say more, wants just not to be so sad. I wonder, if I bring Caitlin home, if it would change anything, or if the Banks family machine is permanently broken.

I go up to my room, grab some clean clothes then head to the shower, where thoughts and images of Gabby rather than Charlotte fill my mind and occupy my right hand. By the time I return to my room, Tim's there waiting for me. He's staring at my blank computer screen.

"Hey, why is your Mac shut off? If I had a machine like this, I'd never leave it!" Tim says. "You're never online anymore. And I know it's not because you've been studying."

I stare at Tim blankly.

"Carson, what's with you?" he asks, interested, not angry.

"I'm just trying not to be online as much," I say, hoping I don't need to explain the real reason for my Internet avoidance. I start saying, 'I'm looking for Caitlin,' but that excuse only fools myself for so many photos. I'm not addicted, but I'm detoxing my mind and Mac anyway.

He laughs. "So this is why you didn't answer an IM for the past two days."

"I'm just a call or text away."

"I hate talking on the phone, and you know I don't text," he reminds me. "How will I ever split the atom if my hands are all messed up from text-related injuries?"

I just laugh. The real reason Tim doesn't text is the reason he doesn't do many things—his size. Fact is, while his stubby, fat fingers work fine for typing, they fail at texting.

"Your Mac is your life. I would kill to have a machine that fine," he says. While my Mac is older, I got it when Dad was working, so it's loaded with every option, including Tim's envy.

"Well, maybe I need to change my life," I crack.

Tim readjusts his glasses, but not his thoughts as he says, "I don't believe you, Carson."

"Well, that's the great thing about being friends, Tim. We trust each other, so we don't need to tell the truth," I say. Like I let him lie about why he doesn't text, it allows me to not feel bad about hiding Gabby from him. We'd never say this out loud, but underneath, it's understood.

"Well, let's hang out together some time like we used to, okay?" he says, a little hurt.

"Quality time, like this." I reach over for the ACT study guide.

"So, what's really going on with you?" Tim asks as he pulls out his study guide.

"What do you mean?"

"You're never around," Tim says, sounding sad.

"Like you, Tim, I'm just really busy." Tim and I have a shared past, but we both know, yet never say, we will probably have a hard time staying friends after he leaves for college. The distance between two points is a catalyst. It remains the same, but it changes everything.

"Okay," he says. I bet that if we were girls, we'd have some teary-eyed declaring of our best friends forever status. Instead, we say little, accept a lot and move on with our lives.

I let 'okay' be the last word and open the study guide. The ACT shapes my future by testing what I've learned in the past. As I read the first practice 'define this word' question, I wonder what explains a person most — their past, present, or future? Thinking about Caitlin, I know the answer is simple. It's not what you've done that defines you, but what you dream.

Chapter Thirteen

Wednesday, November 10th

"Do you understand now?" Gabby stares me down like she might a ref after a bad call.

I respond using my lips the same way I've been using them the past hour, by kissing hers. We're in the back seat of her vehicle—a newish white Chevy Tahoe SUV—parked in another unfinished Fenton subdivision. The windows are fogged up as I try to clear my head about the reasons Gabby wants us to stay a secret. Keeping secrets is another area where I excel.

"That's why my dad can't know," she repeats for a third time. There's fear in her eyes and voice. "He and my mom, they went through a lot of shit. He doesn't want that for me."

"I understand," I lie. I don't understand her father's prohibition against her dating someone like me, especially after learning that Gabby's mom is white. A mom she mentioned this one time, but never before and somehow, I suspect, never again.

"It's not personal, Carson, really," she says, trying to laugh. "It's just so complicated."

"I understand," is the latest lie to slip easily off my tongue.

"He's protecting me," she says. "He says we have enough problems living out in Fenton without calling attention. But it's also focusing on my goals."

"What do you mean?"

"He wants my focus on athletics, which means not wasting time with distractions like dating," she continues, looking embarrassed. "I don't think anybody I went out with—black, white, or blue—would measure up to his standards. He means they don't measure up to him."

"Well, I bet he's tall," I crack.

"He's like six eight."

"Six eight! I don't mind not meeting him. He'd crack my head like an egg."

"He's not a person you ever want to disappoint." She sounds dead serious.

"So did your dad play basketball, too?"

"He's got more trophies than a Saginaw Street pawn shop!"

"Did he make the pros?" I ask.

"He should have, but he got hurt his sophomore year in college. In high school, he was all-state and had a free ride to UCLA." She sounds suddenly sad. "He tore up his knee something terrible. He'd try to come back, but his knee always let him down. I guess that's why I can't."

"Let him down?"

"I don't know about you, Carson, but sometimes I feel like I'm carrying the weight of my dad's dreams," she says. "The good thing, though, is they are my dreams now."

"So, Gabrielle Gibson, what do you want to be when you grow up?"

"My dream? My dream would be to be the first woman to play in the NBA, but I know that's a fantasy, not a goal," she says, then laughs it aside. I admire how she can tell the difference between the two. "I want to win a scholarship to a California college in basketball, volleyball and track. I want to make all-American then go to the Olympics as the first woman to compete in three sports. I want to win three gold medals and—"

"It sounds like you've not really thought this out," I joke. "Why California?"

"I've lived in cold, damp, gray Michigan all my life," she says. "I want to watch the sunset while walking on a California beach, like my dad never got to. I know, stupid, right?"

"I hope that dream comes true." I hate that I feel like I'm lying to her in some way. Look where Caitlin's dreams got her? Maybe if everything—

"I love this song!" Gabby reaches to the dash and turns up the radio. "Just listen."

Yet, even as I'm just where I want to be—having this smart, beautiful, successful girl in my arms—I can't stop thinking about Caitlin. Not just because I still don't know where she is, but because I remember *who* she was. All this talk of dreams gets me thinking about Caitlin's ambitions of stardom, despite an outstanding lack of talent. Maybe the porn-site owners haven't found Caitlin yet for me, but I shouldn't be so surprised that she found them.

I'd sneak into her room when I was in junior high to use her computer—my parents had locked a filter on mine I'd not yet cracked—and I found a notebook filled with different versions of her autograph. She'd wear gold-rimmed, expensive sunglasses no matter the weather, and I don't think it was to hide bloodshot eyes. Caitlin drank, dropped X, smoked weed, but her real drug of choice was celebrity. She'd watch every reality TV show and talk about trying out for all of them. The only thing Caitlin had wanted was to be the person on the screen, not staring at it.

"I don't need to ask you, do I?" Gabby says when the song ends. "You want to be a writer."

"More than anything in the world," I reply with a truth so deep that it hurts.

She turns down the volume and leans against me. "How is your story coming?"

"It's a series of stories that will make a novel."

"Autumn's going to make it?" It's cool Gabby likes my story, but it's her body I'd prefer she be interested in exploring. I'm curious why she's so interested in Autumn but am afraid to ask.

"Like I said, I don't know yet," I answer.

"I want a happy ending, and you should know I don't like not getting what I want."

"That's because you love to win," I tease.

"No, Carson, it's because I hate to lose."

"But just because you don't win, doesn't mean you're a loser."

"That's why I was so messed up at Charlotte's party," she says. "That's maybe why—"

"Is that the only reason you kissed me? Because you felt like a loser?"

"Look, Carson. I'm not good at this," she says very slowly in a whisper. "I'm good out there on the hardwood floor, but I don't know a lot about this stuff." She kisses me softly.

"I like this stuff."

"Not just doing stuff, even talking about it. It makes me feel like I'm not in control."

"Well, you took control of me that night!" I remind her.

"The reason I never approached you, after you broke up with Thien, was because of Charlotte. I know you liked her. Everybody knew that. So as long as she was available, you'd always want her, right?" she asks.

"Maybe," I mutter. I'm amazed, and a little scared, at how Gabby sees the real me.

"When she and Josh hooked up, I figured I had a chance. I went to the creative writing club even though the most creative thing I do is a head fake. I wanted to know you, but when I heard your story, I knew I *needed* to know you. I guessed that you'd be at Charlotte's party, so I pushed myself to go," she continued. "Then I saw you but was still too afraid to talk to you."

"Why? I'm so nice," I joke.

"The worst feeling on the basketball court isn't missing a shot, but a blocked shot. I hate being rejected," she says in a voice that sounds so vulnerable, innocent yet experienced.

"Me too, although you'd think with all of my experience that—"

"Listen, I'm serious," she says, then cuts me off with a kiss. My head is still spinning when she adds, "So, I did what I never do on the court. I made a desperate shot way out of my range."

"She shoots. She scores!" I use my overexcited sports announcer voice, following up with a fake crowd sound. For a second, I imagine the loud noises Gabby will make during sex.

"So, if you think about it, there's really one person who set all this in motion," she says, moving closer. "I know you hate Josh, but you really should thank him."

"For what?"

"For us," Gabby says as she lifts off her shirt. We kiss as I fumble with her bra. She unhooks it. As I move my mouth onto her nipples, she rubs my hair. While there's music from the radio, there's no screaming or yelling my name. It's church silence. What am I doing wrong?

Unlike Thien, who played defense, Gabby's not shy about her body, only her words. She unsnaps my jeans, but when I try to do the same, she bats my hands away. "Slow down," she says. Yet even as she says those words, she's got me in her left hand and I'm ready to explode.

I try to push down my pants, but she's not having it. I lean in, put my mouth against her ear and breathe heavily. I start to talk. "Come on. Give it me. Don't you want my —"

She pulls her hand away. "Carson, shut up," she whispers. Why isn't she pulling off her clothes? Why isn't she acting like she's supposed to?

"What's wrong, Gabby?" With my mouth by her left ear, I bite down.

"Fuck! That hurt!" She pulls away from me. "Carson, what's your problem?"

She finally screamed, but not in ecstasy. This is wrong, all wrong. "What's yours?"

She moves back toward me. "Carson, just slow down, okay?"

Before I can answer, her left hand is back in my pants. I close my eyes, but wonder if I'm asleep because it's more like a dream than my daily life. In the cramped back seat of this SUV, the big distance between what I have and what I want disappears.

Chapter Fourteen

Excerpt from Autumn's Fall
'Halloween Horror'

"Can't you please shut up, Autumn?" Autumn's mother shouted, but as always, Autumn didn't listen. Instead, she continued to rant on her cell to who knew who about what a bitch her mom was, what a pain in the ass her kid brother was and how her senior year sucked. She listed all of her failures at school and how they were all someone else's fault. August didn't understand why Autumn couldn't be happy with what she had, or why she always wanted more.

"Mom, don't worry. It's not that important," August said. His mom can't tell he's lying. She's used to Autumn lying all the time, so she's put all of her faith in her youngest child.

"No, you're a freshman in high school. This is most certainly your last Halloween," August's mom said to him, before turning toward Autumn to say, "Seniors aren't supposed to do this. Seniors should have better things to do, like looking for a job, studying for classes so they don't flunk out of high school, cleaning their room, helping out their grandma more, or—"

"Shut up!" Autumn shouted at her mom, then clicked the phone.

"Watch your mouth, young lady," her mom said, sounding more shocked than hurt.

"If you haven't noticed, Mommy, I'm not a lady," Autumn said as her ruby red high heels clicked across the kitchen linoleum. Rather than going upstairs, Autumn stopped in front of a large mirror in the hallway and took selfies of her Halloween costume, though it wasn't much different from her regular attire. The outfit was more black fishnet than fabric.

"August, I've just been so busy with my mother, with work, everything," his mom said to him instead of saying 'I'm sorry'. "Why don't you stay home with me and your dad tonight?"

"Now there's a party, big brother," Autumn shouted. "A drunk dad and a—"

"That's it!" August's mom shouted. "If you say another word…"

Autumn clicked back into the kitchen. "You want to finish that sentence?"

August could tell his mom was exhausted and defeated, so he said, "Little sister, please."

"Okay. For you, big brother," she said, then headed back to the mirror. August moved to the door when the doorbell rang. After opening it, he slumped in defeat.

"It's not trick or treat. It's Dwayne," August said, but nobody laughed. August thought with his crappy freshman year, his grandma's illness and Autumn, nobody except Autumn laughed in their house anymore. Whatever drugs Autumn consumed had to be the cause.

"Autumn, let's go!" Dwayne said as he stuck his biker boots in the door. After the havoc of homecoming, Dwayne was supposed to be barred from the house, but August knew better. When he was up late at night writing, he saw Dwayne's motorcycle parked outside.

"Almost," Autumn said, as she admired herself in the mirror. August noticed that with his mom around, Dwayne didn't launch into his litany of how hot Autumn looked, although no doubt Autumn could suffer some heavy withdrawal if she went without her flattery fix.

With Dwayne halfway in the door, the unseasonably cold Michigan air pushed inside. August smiled seconds later when he heard the click of the furnace coming on and knew Mr. Innocent would race to the heat vent. But the dog made a detour to bark and snap at Dwayne.

"Somebody oughta kill that rat," Dwayne said, as Mr. Innocent mixed growls with barks. Dwayne swung at the dog with the bag he was carrying. It was Autumn's black bag with the Playboy logo on it. Dwayne was going trick or treating with Autumn, but for August, Dwayne was all trick, no treat.

"Hey, knock it off," August yelled at Dwayne.

"Who do you think you're talking to, little man?" Dwayne shouted back.

"Dwayne, don't pick on my brother," Autumn snapped at Dwayne, who glared at August.

"Mr. Innocent, come here," August shouted. The dog paused for a second, then came as he'd been told. Like owner, like dog, August thought.

"I'm out, big brother," Autumn said, patting August as she walked past him. His head filled with his zitty face that made him want to die in shame most every day. How could his sister be so beautiful, August wondered, while he was such an ugly troll?

"I want you home on time for once, young lady," August's mom said as her daughter passed by. "You have the ACT to study for, you know."

Autumn turned on her heel, then said, "I'm not studying for some stupid test."

"With your grades, you'll need a good score to get into college and—"

"I'm not going to college," Autumn said, then laughed—her stoned laugh.

"What do you plan to do with yourself?" August's mom asked

"Be fucking famous!" Autumn shouted over the sound of the dog barking and her heels clicking as she walked through the kitchen and out into the night with Dwayne. When August stared at Dwayne, he thought it wasn't Halloween night. It was still Devil's night.

* * * *

"Mr. Innocent?" August called out, but his dog didn't answer. Normally curled up on his bed or by the heat vent when August woke up each morning, the dog was missing.

August put on one of the few pairs of jeans that fit his growth-spurt-challenged body and started walking through the house calling the dog's name. Nothing. The back door was locked, and there was no note. Both of his parents were at work. He called again, louder. Nothing.

As he walked back toward his room, he heard a cough from Autumn's room. A cough quickly followed by a scream. August ran toward the door. The always-locked door.

"Autumn, what's wrong?" he shouted loudly, then knocked even louder.

"Shit," he heard Autumn say, then heard the lock click open. He heard a strange sound, his sister Autumn crying, but another sound was stranger. Silence when he saw Mr. Innocent in her room, but he didn't hear the dog barking. August took a tentative step inside the chaotic room with clothes, magazines, jewelry and more clothes scattered everywhere.

And Autumn's Playboy logo bag. The bag August had seen Dwayne with last night.

And next to the bag were piles of candy wrappers.

Hershey's dark chocolate—candy for kids, poison for dogs.

And next to the bag and the wrappers was Mr. Innocent.

August didn't remember when Mr. Innocent had left his room for Autumn's room. He didn't know the history. He just felt the fear of the here and now.

When the furnace clicked on and the dog didn't move, August joined his sister in tears as the chill of the morning, grief and loss iced through his veins.

"August, I don't know what to say," Autumn cried.

August screamed in agony as he lay next to Mr. Innocent.

"I didn't know," she said.

August tried to form words, but no verbs or noun left his throat. The screaming wouldn't allow it. "If I find out that Dwayne had anything to do with this, he is so done."

August looked at the bag, the dog, then up at his sister. "Did you?"

Autumn slapped her brother. He was already crying, so she must have figured, why not add to the pain? "I would never do anything to hurt you. You're the only one in this house who cares about me. If I disappeared tomorrow, they wouldn't even come looking, but you would."

"Only to the end of the earth."

Which made Autumn smile, depositing his hurt in another place if only for a second. August knew if his sister kept on her path, she'd be as dead as Mr. Innocent. He had to protect Autumn from her own worst enemy — the person she stared at incessantly in the mirror, the person she photographed as if she was afraid she'd forget what she looked like — herself.

Chapter Fifteen

Thursday, November 18th
Creative writing club meeting

August knew if his sister kept on her path, she'd be as dead as Mr. Innocent. He had to protect Autumn from her own worst enemy – the person she stared at incessantly in the mirror, the person she photographed as if she was afraid she'd forget what she looked like – herself.

"Before we discuss this story, there's something I must mention," Dr. Draper says as she passes a piece of paper around. "This is a short story and poetry contest that the club will be sponsoring. Submissions are due at our January meeting, and then we'll announce the winners at our February meeting. In addition to a small cash prize, the winning story and poem will be the first two entries in the literary magazine, a magazine which we've yet to discuss."

"I'd be happy to edit it for you, Dr. Draper," Kirk says. I wonder if he notices I roll my eyes whenever he opens his big mouth or shows off his brown nose.

"Kirk, thank you for the offer, but I think it best that we have one of the juniors or sophomores take on that role so we can build a base for next year."

Inside, I cry out that famous sports cliché — down goes Frazier, down goes Frazier!

"That's okay. I don't have time anyway, with all my college applications," Kirk says, trying to save pompous face. And my face is smiling at the brain bully getting a little taste.

"What college do you plan on attending, Kirk?" Dr. Draper asks.

I swallow my sighs. I don't want to hear about Kirk's college plans or life story. I want to hear what people thought about my story. She's holding it in her hands, but she won't let it go as the clock on the wall keeps clicking away. This clock seems to be ticking slower than normal, while my own timepiece is running fast. I finished the story at school this morning because I can barely find time to write with my old responsibilities and my ones with Gabby. Since I'm rarely online, I barely talk to Tim or my other friends. Everybody else thinks I'm a ghost because they never see me, yet they know I'm around. I'm not undead, I'm living, for once.

"Northwestern is a great school," I hear Candy say. "I thought about applying there, but I really want to go to Columbia. Chicago is the second city. New York is the first."

"Live from New York, it's Candy Tanner!" I shout, mostly to laughs.

Candy purses her dry, thin lips as if auditioning for a most annoyed person in the world contest.

"What about you, Carson?" Dr. Draper asks.

I ponder for a second. This is creative writing, so I could spin a fanciful tale of my future, except when thinking about it, I can barely tell the difference anymore between fact and fiction, between dreams and wishful thinking.

"I'm not sure. I might stay here and go to Baker College at first."

"Good luck with that, Carson. Baker College is so hard to get into," Kirk says. "The admissions policy is a pulse and a checkbook."

I hate Kirk. I hate his put-downs, but laugh anyway. Funny is funny.

"What about you, Charlotte?" Dr. Draper asks.

"Oberlin and Drake are our top choices," she answers while staring at Josh. Unlike the admissions policy of a pulse and checkbook, I know from college guides how hard those schools are to get into and how expensive they are — the very definition of dream schools.

As the other seniors talk about their plans, I'm looking at my Chucks. They remind me of Gabby and me — one black, one white. She wears the same. It's cool to have an inside joke.

"Comments on our first story?" Silence, except for the sound of a million paper cuts on my skin. When no one speaks up, Dr. Draper clears her throat. "Does anyone want to read aloud?"

Why didn't she just say, 'Josh, please descend from the heavens'?

I sit there with a stupid fake smile plastered on my face as Josh reads more from 'Searching for a Heart', which he announces is too big and important a story not to be a novel. He says the only problem is he has two other stories he's working on and can't decide if those are short stories or another novel. Oh, the hardship and agony of a young genius.

As Josh reads, I do my best to listen out of politeness, even if every ideal image, adroit drop of dialog and fantastically fancy sentence slams against my skull like Thor's hammer.

After Josh finishes almost twenty minutes later, Charlotte's first to comment, but slavish praise isn't a comment. I keep the fake smile plastered on my face as I feel anger deep inside.

After Kirk adds the final layer of icing on Josh's compliment cake, Dr. Draper starts the next piece — yet another rhyme about razor blades and roses, I suspect from the tortured poetic souls of the freshman girls. I've stopped caring what anybody thinks, but I also understand why I write fiction. It seems the only two things I'm good at are lying and failing. I failed as a writer and have so far failed in finding my sister. You lose, you lose.

Dr. Draper finishes the emo ode and starts the discussion, which is lively. I do a fake cough then excuse myself and race my non-athletic body to the journalism office. Some of the yearbook staff are still working, so I find a computer as far away as I can. I use the trick Tim taught me to pass the school's filter to get to my email and also visit a page I used to visit almost every day for a year — Caitlin's first shot at fame. Her Facebook page. The activity date stays stuck like some broken clock — and it fits, since in many ways time stopped for all of us on the day before she left. It's like a snapshot of her life three years ago. Well, being Caitlin, snapshot is the right word.

I don't even need to log on. Caitlin always had her page set to public — to look at her pictures. In addition to the tagged photos folder, there are three folders — My pix, Friendz and Modeling. There's not a folder for family, as if we didn't exist.

Each of the folders contains over one thousand photos, yet even as I page through them, I think how they'll all be the same. In the pictures, her face has three expressions — her lips kissing the camera, her mouth open to show off her tongue stud or no expression because while her body is revealed, her eyes are hidden behind sunglasses. One photo says it all. Caitlin flanked by two guys on each side. She's wearing her favorite attention-getting, piss off Dad outfit — a tight gold low-cut top that seems to be in most of the partying photos. In this photo, she's with a white guy and a black guy in their twenties. Each has a hand pressed against the side of Caitlin's breasts to produce even more cleavage than usual, although it's hard to see with the bottle of Grey Goose between her breasts. Her eyes are wild red, not sky blue. But her smile says it all — look at me.

And people did. This photo, like most of the others, has almost a hundred comments. I used to overhear Caitlin on the phone complaining to friends if they didn't comment on her photos or vids. I'm deep into Caitlin's past when an email arrives from one of the porn sites I wrote. I gave up the sister angle and tried thinking like a porn producer. It's all about the money. I asked if the girl in the pictures had any DVDs I could buy. The email tells me the model's name is Callie Bangs. She's only in one DVD, but would I like to sign up for her webcam?

I clear the cache and history, and race for my car. I'm heading home, and maybe my sister will be coming home with me someday very soon. This discovery leads not to certainty, but just to more questions. Not just the practical ones about how I'll contact her or what I'll say to her, but the hardest question of all. Who will I be talking to—Caitlin Banks or Callie Bangs?

Chapter Sixteen

Thursday, November 25th
Thanksgiving Day

"Are you feeling okay?" Mom asks. Shared sadness weighs heavily over every holiday.

"Just tired." I push aside my half-eaten plate of food. With Carol not home and the extended family spread out over the country, Thanksgiving isn't much of a celebration, because this family doesn't have a lot to be thankful for this year — like last year, and the one before that. We're all dressed up, but with no place good for our hearts to go.

"Girl problems," Dad says, then winks at Mom. They still don't know about Gabby. She's busy with her own family. Somehow that makes me even lonelier than when I had nobody.

"I wish I had girl problems!" I shout. Nobody laughs. Nobody laughs here anymore.

"Girls at your age will only lead to problems," Mom, a teen mom herself, says, then sighs.

"Mom, Dad, can I ask you something?"

"If it's about college, we just don't know. I might be back to work next—" Dad starts.

"Not college." I pause, stiffen my spine and prepare to break their hearts. "Caitlin."

"Why would you spoil Thanksgiving?" Mom asks. "Didn't she ruin enough holidays?"

"Carson, please, don't upset your mother, not today," Dad says softly. He gulps down the beer he'd probably planned to nurse through the meal.

"No, we should talk about her," I counter. "What would happen if she came home?"

There's a long pause. A time standing still pause. It's so quiet I can hear my dad's cheap watch clicking from across the table. Or maybe that's all our hearts beating too loud.

Mom breaks the soft silence. "Honey, Caitlin isn't coming home."

"She can't come home," Dad says. "Not after what she's done."

"Doesn't everyone deserve a second chance?" I ask Mom. I channel Gabby.

"Caitlin used up her second chances," Dad says. "She had two hundred second chances."

"If only we had done something earlier," Mom says.

"It is not your fault. She made her choice!" Dad says, then storms from the table before I confront him with what I've long known, but never said. I heard from the top of the stairs the choice he gave his daughter on Christmas morning—a choice no person should have to make.

"I'm sorry, Mom," I say. In the other room, I hear the fridge, then the bottle open. The second of many, I suspect. "I shouldn't have said anything."

"It's not your fault," she says softly. "It's everybody's fault."

I don't say anything. Instead, I help clean up the table that we all messed up.

* * * *

Up in my room, I hear nothing but silence downstairs. I put on a hoodie, then surrender again to the computer and consider my options, mostly pondering ends and means. My end is simple — contact Caitlin. The means are difficult. I have no way to reach her. Without a credit card, I can't get into her webcam. I found the Callie Bangs Facebook page immediately, but she's not responded to the message I sent, which was simply —

Caitlin, it's your brother Carson. Please contact me.

There's little on her Facebook except nearly nude photos of her newly tattooed arms, the fact that she lives in California and information about what she likes to do in bed. The last login date is two months ago, which sends chills up and down my spine. Two months ago because she's done with *that* life, or two months ago because she's done with *her* life? Like her old Facebook page, this new one prompted hundreds of comments.

Last Thursday, when I Googled her new name, I found more photos, but no way to contact her. Buying a prepaid cell, I called the company, but nobody answered or returned my call. The company selling her is based in California, so I searched online phone books but found nothing. I looked under Callie, Caitlin, even Autumn, and under both Banks and Bangs, but couldn't find an address, phone or email. She's an optical illusion—so close yet still so far.

I'm getting nowhere when I get an IM from Tim. He's bored and wants to get together. As guys, neither of us will admit to missing each other, but that's obviously what's going on. I've not told him about Gabby, but it's time. I'm drowning in secrets heavier than Mom's gravy.

* * * *

"Hey, you want some Dew?" Tim says, offering me a sip from his two-liter almost the second I climb in his Mom's silver Monte Carlo. It's a neat as a marine's boot camp footlocker.

"No thanks," I say, then sip from my travel coffee mug. "So, where to?"

"I don't know. Everything's closed," he says.

"You got gas?"

"I just ate twenty pounds of Thanksgiving dinner. What do you think?"

"I meant gas in the car, a-hole," I crack back.

"Half full," Tim says.

"Half empty," I correct him. "Why don't we just drive?"

He slurps from his two-liter and starts our two-lane drive to nowhere. Along the way, we do our best to crack on each other as much as we crack each other up, the one area where Tim's NHS friends don't excel. Sometimes we get serious, talking about how bad the economy in Michigan is, although lots of people in school like Tim don't seem to think or talk about it as much as I do. But then, Tim's dad still works in some executive job for GM. The white-collar guys keep their jobs. The blue-collar guys like Dad lose theirs. That's probably why Dad wants me to be an engineer. Tim's MIT bound and getting out. No wonder he sees the tank half full.

We drive around Fenton, past all the half-finished subdivisions and nearly deserted strip malls. Just before Tim gets ready to pull on the expressway, I ask him instead to drive toward Silver Lake Road. I direct him into yet another cookie cutter collection of houses. Half are for sale, the other half show Hummers or huge GM SUVs in the driveway. I ask him to slow down by a house with a white Chevy Tahoe covered with Fenton sports bumper stickers in the driveway.

"Who lives here?" Tim asks.

Coffee sip, deep breath, and here we go. "Gabrielle Gibson."

"That tall black girl?" Tim asks and something clicks, what it's like to be Gabby. Tim doesn't say the pretty girl, the athletic girl or the shy, smart girl, but the tall black girl. Tim doesn't have a racist bone in his body so he means nothing. It's just how Fenton sees Gabby.

"Can you pull over?" I ask. Tim finds a spot behind a newish black Dodge Charger.

"What's going on?"

"Can I trust you with a secret?"

He ponders for a second with a puzzled look on his face, then looks toward the house, back at me, then asks while a huge smile taking over, "You're hitting that?"

I pause for a second, then crack a smile of my own when I answer, "I can't say."

"That means you are," he says, then laughs. "Congrats."

"I didn't say I was, but I didn't say I'm not. So, I'm not lying or telling you anything."

"Your moral ground is shakier than cafeteria Jell-O!"

"But, let's say we ran an experiment, and I was romantically involved—not 'hitting that' as you say, Dew boy—with Ms. Gibson. What results might we find?"

"What do you mean?"

I turn from Tim and stare at Gabby's house. "Do you think I'd piss people off?"

"Who cares what other people think?"

I imagine her inside, in her bed. "Okay, what would you think of this?"

"I think it's a mistake," he says, then sips from the Mountain.

My heart skips. I turn back toward Tim. "Because she's black?"

He laughs. "No, because she'd kick your ass if you messed up like you did with Thien."

I laugh back. "Well, it's other physical activities that I'd rather—"

He cuts me off with a loud slurp then says, "Everybody's pairing up but poor, pitiful me."

"Look, why don't you go out with some of the Honor Society girls, like Thien?"

"What? I get your leftovers?"

"She likes you." While I'm worried that Thien might spill our prom secret, I'm more concerned that my best pal spends weekend nights fetching lo mein instead of locking lips.

"You never told me what happened with her," he says. "If I'm not getting any, at least I could live vicariously through you, but no, you're Mr. Too Shy To Talk About It."

"So you really don't know what happened with Thien at the prom last spring?" I ask.

"I figured if you wanted to tell me, you'd share it."

"Thanks," I say then shut up.

"I don't know about you, Carson, but all this talk about girls is driving me crazy."

"We should go." I stare at Gabby's house. "Where to?"

"I bet I know one place that's open," Tim says. "Dort Highway."

"Dort Highway?" Dort Highway is Flint's main street for skin bars.

"Think we could sneak into a strip club?" Tim looks sad when I don't jump on the idea. "I bet you'd find only Flint's worst strippers working a holiday. Not a porn star among them."

I want to smack myself in the face at something so obvious. After getting Tim to promise again not to tell about Gabby, and after he gets me to promise we'll hang out more and hit a strip club on my eighteenth birthday in January, he drives me home in minutes that seem like hours.

I scale the steps like Kong going up the Empire State Building. Screw online avoidance, I need my technology as I search for 'Callie Bangs' along with terms like 'dancer' and 'stripper'. This is indeed a day to give thanks for the bounty of information the Internet brings. Within seconds, my almost three year long search is over as I see the name of the LA strip club where Callie will be next month. California, here I come.

Chapter Seventeen

Friday, December 3rd

"Carson, what are you doing here?" I look up from my notebook and see Charlotte, for once without Josh Brown attached like a golden barnacle to her side. Here is the first home game of the Fenton Lady Tigers with their star player, The Great Gabby. I'm here as a reporter. Sure I am.

Charlotte's with a few friends. She motions for them to keep moving and she sits next to me. I imagined her many times this close, but not this clothed. She wears a big blue hoodie to cover her tiny frame. She's got Josh's class ring on her left thumb. "I'm covering girls' sports."

She doesn't say a word, just nods, smiles. A sly smile. I don't like it.

"Sure, Carson, that's why you're here." The smile turns to a smirk. My face turns red.

"What?" I look down at my deliberately mismatched Chucks.

"It's okay, nobody else knows," Charlotte whispers.

How long will I play this stupid card wearing my worst poker face? "Know what?"

Charlotte leans closer, her hand almost on my leg and her mouth near my ear. "You and her." She points toward the court, where Gabby shoots three pointers during warm-ups. I take Charlotte's hand and put it back by her side. Weeks ago that skin touch would have thrilled me for days.

"I don't know what you're talking about." My eyes no doubt dart back and forth.

"She told me, Carson," Charlotte whispers. I'm angry at Gabby for all of one second, since I told Tim. "And it is so obvious, if you know it, but I think your secret is safe with me."

"When did she tell you?"

Charlotte starts to answer, but then we notice the game is about to start. We stand for the anthem. Candy Tanner, the hammer to my writing club nail, stands in front of the microphone. Everybody's all hand on heart, but if I did that, people would see it bouncing off my chest like Gabby dribbling the ball. I'm not angry that Charlotte knows, but oddly excited. Like it's some sort of vindication after having struck out with Charlotte for years, then having been ejected from the game by Thien, that I'm not a love life loser. I mean, I'd had other make-out partners before, dating back to ninth grade, but they'd all ended too soon. It had been practice for the real thing, except I'd never gotten to the shirts and skins levels or even close. Maybe there's room for only so much sex, and since porn takes up so much of it, the universe takes it from someplace else, which would be the females of Fenton, except Gabby. Gabby slows down my game, but at least I'm on the court. I feel guilty thinking about sex during the national anthem, but I notice Candy sings a second verse. How many are there? The answer appears to be three. Wait, four.

"So, Charlotte, how long have you known?" I say when we sit. Gabby's ready to jump.

"Last year," she says in a pseudo whisper. "After you wrote that story about her, she asked if I knew you. Tennis players gossip like you wouldn't believe." I imagine Gabby in a tight white bright Serena-style outfit and a wide smile on her face as she smashes the ball across the net.

"Then why did she wait until this year?" I so don't understand girls' minds, although thanks to Gabby I am learning some of the finer points of the female anatomy.

"First off, you went to prom with Thien."

Gabby grabs a rebound and starts the fast break up court. "Like that lasted." Charlotte's silent like she's expecting me to say more, and I'm hoping that she doesn't know anything. I can't imagine she does because I don't think she'd want to be sitting this close to me.

"Then after that... Well, you had that other girl." I shrug at the odd expression.

The pass comes back to Gabby, who hits a three off the backboard. The clang matches the sound in my head from Charlotte's puzzling words. "Who do you mean...that other girl?"

Charlotte stares down at the wood bleacher. "Me, Carson. Gabby knew you liked me."

My face blushes brighter red than the Beecher High jerseys. "If only that was mutual."

"I'd heard some things about you." She doesn't end the sentence with 'from Thien'.

"I have quite the reputation as a ladies' man." I laugh. She doesn't make a sound. Now she's like mute Thien and whoever these girls are that Charlotte says talk trash about me.

"Do you want to know the truth?"

Gabby steals a pass and starts for the basket.

"No," I answer, but I know headstrong Charlotte, who stubbornly resisted my every feeble flirtation, clumsy pass or outright straight-ahead requests to go out, is going to tell me.

She moves closer. I wonder where Josh is. He's probably spinning a seamless sonnet. "Girls are just different than guys about...you know. You wanted too much too soon, I heard."

Beecher inbounds the ball and moves up-court. Two quick passes and a shot goes up, except Gabby times her leap perfectly and rejects. The home crowd cheers, except the girls who are here, who I guess want to boo me. *Don't blame me*, I think, *blame Homemade Hos*. The producers who send more email than Nigerian oil barons, but no info on Caitlin aka Callie. Not that it matters anymore since I know where and when to find her, just not how I'll get there.

"Well, I didn't scare Gabby away," I say in the pouty tone of a five year old.

"That's because, I think, she loves you." Charlotte whispers the big three words. On the court, Gabby hits a three pointer. The crowd cheers. I take in the applause as my own.

My shocked hands drop my pen and notebook. "She said that?"

"Like I said, Carson, girls and guys are different. I can tell from how she talked about you," Charlotte says. "It's like when I talk about Josh."

I pick up the pen and notebook, but say nothing about the bard boy wonder. "Carson, we've known each other a long time, right? Since seventh grade, right?" I nod yes to all of this.

"Well, I've known Josh for way longer," she says. "Our parents are in the same country club. They're friends, so..." The only club Dad belongs to is AA.

"How long have the two of you...?" I don't know what phrase to use—been together, hooked up or crushed my dreams. Maybe all of the above. I use her words. "You know."

"This summer, finally," Charlotte stammers, which is odd for such a confident person as she always appears to be. "That's the other reason, Carson, me and you. I wanted Josh only."

I try to pay attention to the game, but the back and forth action makes me dizzy as Charlotte lays down a full court truth press that I didn't ask for and certainly don't need.

"So, look. He and I got together, and now you and Gabby. So, the universe worked it out."

If the universe worked, I think, I wouldn't be developing some elaborate story to tell my parents so I can lie my way to California to rescue my stripper turned minor porn actress sister, or maybe the other way around. I'm unfamiliar with the sex industry career ladder.

"One last thing, Carson." Charlotte's small hand goes hard on my shoulder. She grips it like she does a racket or Josh's hand. *Do not mess this up.* I care about you and Gabby. Whatever got screwed up with Thien, learn from your mistakes. Gabby deserves it."

"It?" I ask Charlotte, but my eyes focus on Gabby running with grace down the court. Charlotte lets go of my shoulder, but I gaze upon Gabby's shoulders. I imagine them sweaty.

Charlotte stands and says, "A happy ending."

One last blush, since that's taken on a whole new meaning in Gabby's hands. Hands that just shot the ball through the hoop. Love turns life turns into nothing but net.

Chapter Eighteen

Monday, December 6th

"Kate, what do you think?" Dad asks Mom, trying to make her play the bad guy.

"I know it's a lot of money, but this is what I want," I say, before Mom gets a chance to speak. "Dad, if you go back to work next year like you think, then it won't even be an issue."

"Carson, you know because of Caitlin that—" she starts, but I don't want to hear it.

"Let me go to California over Christmas break. Give this to me as a combo Christmas, birthday and graduation burrito," I plead. I hide my balled up, frustrated fist under the kitchen table, the location for serious talks like this.

"How much is the plane ticket?" Dad asks again. Like him, I've had no success at finding a job. It seems no one in Fenton wants to hire someone with no experience who needs two to three nights a week off so they can cover sports. What kind of world is that?

"I checked online. It's four hundred and fifty dollars from Detroit to San Diego," I explain, trying to sound confident and mature. "I'll leave Christmas night and come back Wednesday midday."

"I know your sister would like to see you since she can't come home for Christmas," Mom says. She, of course, doesn't know Carol isn't the only sister I plan to see in CA.

"We could drive. What about that?" Dad asks. "You and your old man on a road trip?"

"I'd love to, but I don't have time." I feel guilty about lying so much. This is what Caitlin did—lied about money, lied about where she was going and where she had been.

"Carson, I just don't know about you making a trip like this alone," Hover Mom says.

"Look, I'm not Caitlin. I'm Carson. You can trust me." The furnace clicks on, loudly.

"But you'd be missing part of Christmas with us," Mom says.

"Mom, we all know Christmas has never been the same since—" I start.

Dad cuts me off. "It's not about trust, Carson. It's about the money. We don't have it."

"I wouldn't ask unless it was really important. I just need to get out of Michigan. Get away from this cold weather. Get away from everything going on at school." Truth. Lie. Lie. Lie.

"Carol said it was eighty degrees in San Diego on Sunday," Mom says. Mom's melting but Dad's lips are frozen shut.

"Look, if you do this, Mom, Dad, I won't ask for anything again."

"I don't understand why this is so important." Dad says. He actually scratches his head to communicate his confusion. "What are you hiding?"

"Nothing." Or, in other words, everything.

"Then what is it?" Mom wants to agree, but Caitlin busted all trust in this household.

"I know it's hard. I don't ask for much. Mom, you know what's it's like to dream big."

They stare at each other, then at me. I look for eye or hand signals. Someone will blink.

"Fine," Dad says after a pause that seemed to last hours, not seconds. "Now, how about watching Monday Night Football with your dad like we used to?

"I'd love to, but," I start, thinking about plans already made with Gabby for tonight, as well as my need to finish writing the next part of *Autumn's Fall*.

"But?"

"But I gotta run over to Tim's first," I lie. "I'll catch the second half."

"By the second half, the Lions will be down by twenty," he says. "Come on, son."

They just gave me a big thing—this is a small thing I can do, even if for this family, I'm about to do the biggest. "Okay, maybe you should try to get a job coaching the Lions," I suggest.

"No, that's a broken machine even your old man can't repair," he says as I head upstairs. He doesn't know that in a few weeks, when I bring Caitlin home with me, the Banks family will be fixed.

* * * *

"I got some good news and bad news," I tell Gabby as I hold the phone tightly. I lie on my bed, eyes closed, the image of her face in front of me.

"It's always something with you, Carson Banks, always something," she says.

"Bad news is I can't see you tonight. I have to spend time with my dad."

"Having suffered through eighteen years of father-daughter bonding, I feel your pain."

"Amen," I say, then laugh, but I'd rather ask Gabby about her mom and why she barely mentions her. I'd like to ask a million things about her life, but it seems whenever we're together, we don't talk much. We can't seem to keep our hands off each other.

"Okay, I don't like it, but I accept it," she says. I wish I could feel the same about sex — or lack thereof. Maybe Gabby's one of these 'everything but' girls. I don't know because she won't talk. She's like an artist. She just draws lines.

"You know my birthday's coming up."

She laughs. "I've heard something to that effect, like every day for a month."

"Maybe I could have something special for my birthday."

"What do you have in mind?" she purrs back.

"Maybe we could strip down to our birthday suits."

She sighs, laughs, I hope with, not at me. "The good news?"

"I'm going to California over Christmas. Isn't that cool?"

There's a pause. Awkward. Sad? Angry? "You'll be back for my holiday tourney?"

"I'm leaving Saturday and back on Wednesday. I wouldn't miss you winning the finals of the holiday tournament for anything in this world. I want to see that trophy held high over your pretty face."

"I wish I could go with you," she says in that vulnerable voice that always gets me.

I don't say anything.

"But because of the tourney, I'd better not even think about it," she concludes.

"Okay, I understand," I say, feeling like I dodged a bullet.

"Some other time, maybe," she says. "You know that's my dream — to go to California."

"You know what my dream is?" I ask.

She doesn't answer.

"My face between your legs," I whisper. More silence. "Well? What do you think?"

"What do you think that would be like?" she whispers. "Paint the scene, writer boy."

I start talking, but my breathing grows heavy. She responds in kind. I keep talking softer, she keeps breathing louder, unlike when we're in the car or on the sofa at her house. Pretty soon I'm holding the phone with one hand. I wonder if she's doing the same.

"Let me hear it, Carson."

It takes less than a minute more of vocal inspiration. After a few seconds, I return to the phone, but before I can speak, she says, "Feel better now?"

"And how."

"I'll see you soon," she whispers, then kisses me through the phone.

"Well, maybe then it will be your turn, Gabby," I purr.

"I don't know about that." That makes two of us. I'm clueless how to return the favor or even if she wants me to. My pants end up at my ankles, hers remain locked at her waist.

"Gabby, I'd be happy to lend a helping hand."

She laughs, but it sounds different from normal. Maybe a nervous laugh. "Like I said, I don't know about that."

We talk a little more about nothing, but each second with her seems like everything. I want to say 'I love you', but instead I just say goodbye. I wonder what she wants to say to me. She just talked dirty through phone sex, but in person, she rarely makes a sound. Is it her or me?

But mostly I wonder what she wants. Before I head downstairs to bond with Dad, I jump online. I kick past the lies of porn sites and look for some truth about how to make Gabby happy.

Chapter Nineteen

Excerpt from Autumn's Fall
'Thanksgiving Threats'

"Are you coming to dinner?" Autumn's mother yelled as she banged on the locked door.

"Leave me alone!" Autumn shouted back.

The shouting was loud enough for everyone seated around the table for Thanksgiving dinner to hear. Amber was home from her senior year in college, royally dressed in Boston College apparel. While everybody wanted Grandma to come to dinner, she was just too weak. Instead, they all spent the morning at her house. A house that was mostly clean and tidy, which amazed everyone, since cleaning her grandma's house was the only task that Autumn did without complaint and with some competence, although it still wasn't clean enough for August's mom. Instead of visiting, August did tasks like gathering up recycling and sorting mail. Autumn wanted to help him, but her mom made her clean the bathroom.

"Hurry up. The dinner is getting cold and the Lions kick off in an hour," August's dad yelled. His dad yelled a lot, although lately he was yelling less at Autumn. You can't scream at someone if you don't see them. Dad's solution to the Autumn problem seemed to be abandoning her before she did the same to the rest of the family. His silence was deafening.

"Let me talk to her," August shouted, then headed upstairs.

"Why bother?" Amber asked, then shook her head, yet not a single hair fell out of place, it would seem. "Honestly, Daddy, I don't know why you and Mom put up with her."

"She's our daughter," August's dad answered, then finished another beer.

"Then maybe she should act like one," Amber said. "Or at least like a human being."

August rose from the table so he could talk to one sister and avoid talking to another.

* * * *

"Autumn, open the door," August begged. He didn't pound. He let his words speak, which was odd since he'd not spoken much to Autumn since Halloween, despite her attempts. August—grief-stricken over the loss of Mr. Innocent—felt loneliness drag on him like leg chains.

"Go away," Autumn replied.

"No, you need to talk with me," August said. "I'm ready to talk to you."

A moment passed. Downstairs, August heard Amber talking to, not with, their parents about her grand plans after she graduated from college in the spring.

The door clicked, and August's heart dropped. That clicking sound of the lock, his keyboard, his camera, his phone, his TV remote, his everything, sent a shiver down his spine. He couldn't shake the memory of the clicking sound of the furnace and his dog rushing to him.

"What do you want?" Autumn asked as she opened the door just an inch.

"Let me in," August said.

"No," she said.

"Please come downstairs. It's Thanksgiving," August pleaded.

"What do I have to be thankful for? Answer me that," Autumn said. "I'm a failure at everything I do. Amber is perfect, and all I do is fail. School. Being famous. Everything."

"Your family is here," August said.

"They're your family, August, not mine," she said as she cracked the door another inch.

August stepped closer, leaning in toward the void. "Come on, please, Autumn? It will be Amber's last Thanksgiving at home, maybe for a while. You know that, right?"

Autumn said nothing because she knew nothing about Amber's plans. Whenever her parents talked about Amber, Autumn turned up the volume or left the room. This time, though, she heard. And she said, "In that case, let's break out the Cristal and celebrate!"

"Autumn, please," August begged.

"Listen, big brother, about your dog," she started.

"Mr. Innocent, say his name," he snapped.

"About Mr. Innocent... Like I told you, I'm so sorry, really. I know you hear me say that 'I'm sorry' crap all the time to the folks, but believe me, I mean it this time. I am so, so sorry."

August tried to remember back to a time when Autumn's mouth moving didn't equal a lie, but his memory was not that good. "I forgave you," he said. You forgave family. It was a given.

"Dwayne's toast," Autumn said, opening the door a little more.

"Why did he poison my dog?" August pleaded, but Autumn didn't answer.

Autumn finally said, "I told him I never wanted to see him again. I did that for you, too."

"Thanks." August wondered why that should matter, because he could tell all along that Dwayne, like Andy, like Austin, like all of the men before Dwayne... They didn't mean anything to her. August sensed that even with these boyfriends, Autumn felt as lonely as he did all the time.

"Let me put on some nice clothes, and I'll be down in a while," Autumn said softly.

August stepped closer. "You sure have a lot of nice new clothes, lots of designer stuff."

Autumn laughed, then said, "Well, Dwayne was pretty good about buying me stuff."

"Dwayne was a punk, a loser, a nothing," August snapped.

"Whatever," she said, leaving the door unguarded. August pushed his way inside.

"Hey, big brother, what are you—"

"I found the credit card past due bills today at Grandma's," August said in a whisper.

"What do you mean?"

"One of Grandma's credit cards had charges for Victoria's Secret," August said. "I don't think a sixty-five-year-old woman with breast cancer shops there, do you?"

Autumn moved back, leaned against one of her full-size mirrors, but said nothing.

"Autumn, how could you do this to Grandma?" August asked.

"What are you going to do?" Autumn asked instead of answering his question.

"I don't know," he said. He wanted to add, I'm fourteen years old and I don't know what to do about anything, let alone something this wrong.

"Don't tell them. They'll kill me," she said.

"I thought you said they would never kill you or abandon you," he reminded her.

"This... This would be worse than either of those things."

"How much? How many?"

"About five large," she replied, but August looked confused. "Five thousand dollars."

"You bought five thousand dollars worth of clothes." August closed the door behind them. The gesture implied the intent — this was going to be their secret.

"I don't want to talk about it and you're not to mention it either. You hear me?"

"Grandma doesn't have that kind of money," August said, almost back to tears.

"I know."

"What were you thinking?"

"I wasn't," Autumn said. "So, what are you going to do?"

"Promise you'll stop," August said, and Autumn nodded. "If you do it again, I'll tell."

She dumped the contents of her purse—money, mirrors, makeup, cigarettes, lighters, condoms and gum—onto her desk. She took red-handled scissors from her desk and held them against the credit card. August guessed that, like the trust for his sister, the cards would be shredded.

"I'm going downstairs," August said sadly. He knew it was impossible to celebrate or give thanks for anything. He was walking downstairs, but Autumn was descending even more.

"Are you angry at me?" Autumn asked. August started out of the door.

"I'm just disappointed," he said as he walked away. Walking away was his only choice.

"She'll be down in a while," August said when he returned to the table.

"About damn time," his dad said. Minutes passed and Dad decided to start the meal without Autumn. Conversation covered all the normal topics—GM, crime in Flint, Mom's latest job selling furniture and a recounting of Amber's academic and social achievements.

"Autumn!" August's mom shouted suddenly. All eyes turned to Autumn on the stairs. She wore a short black dress, tall boots, and carried her Playboy logo bag. Behind her were two red suitcases.

"I came down to say goodbye," Autumn said at the bottom of the stairs.

"Autumn, just sit down for dinner," August's mom said.

"I'm leaving, tonight," Autumn said, totally without emotion.

"What are you talking about?" Amber asked, sounding almost bored.

"I'm moving to New York to be a model," Autumn answered.

"Honey, dear, I think that's a mistake," their mom said quite calmly, considering she was crushing her daughter's dreams. August couldn't help but notice Amber's smirking face.

"There's a huge surprise. Autumn making a mistake and you pointing it out," Autumn said, her tone flatlining. August's dad appeared paralyzed.

"That kind of talking isn't helping," her mom added. "I'm just saying that—"

"Saying that I don't know what I'm doing, saying that I'm a fuck-up," Autumn continued. "Well, it takes one to know one."

"That's enough," her mom said.

"Mom, just say that part of this is your fault that I'm so screwed up," Autumn begged. "Tell me you could have done things better. Tell me just one time that you made a mistake."

Autumn's mom remained silent, like the sky gets before a big storm roars across.

"I can't live here anymore," Autumn said, more sad than angry. August thought it was as if she spoke a language where everybody heard what they wanted. His parents heard she was leaving because she hated them, while Amber probably thought it only proved once again that she was the best daughter, but only August heard the truth—Autumn's leaving was not a promise or a threat. It was not even an act of anger. It was an act of mercy.

Chapter Twenty

Thursday, December 16th
Creative writing club meeting

"I can't live here anymore," Autumn said, more sad than angry. August thought it was as if she spoke a language where everybody heard what they wanted. His parents heard she was leaving because she hated them, while Amber probably thought it only proved once again that she was the best daughter, but only August heard the truth – Autumn's leaving was not a promise or a threat. It was not even an act of anger. It was an act of mercy.

"Anybody?" Dr. Draper asks after she finishes reading more from *Autumn's Fall*. There's time for people to comment since Josh isn't at this meeting, which also means no Charlotte. Gabby's here, but sits across from me. I wonder if she notices me tense up when I see Kirk open his mouth. For the first time in my life, I wish Josh were around. If Josh were here, then he'd have been reading his perfect story rather than me having to listen to Kirk attack mine.

"Wow, where do I start?" Kirk says. He's got a shark smile on his face, a gleam in his eyes and bullets ready to fire from his mouth. "This story reinforces the stereotype that teens are moody and identify only with characters who share these traits. The characters read like they've been recycled from bad teen novels, but with more depravity. But all of this could be forgiven except for the Autumn character. The author neglects to show her positive qualities. The focus is only on her drama. How is anybody supposed to care about this pathetic girl?"

I'm turning the chair beneath me to sawdust, grinding my fingers into it. Poor Caitlin would be so jealous if she could see me now. She always wanted to be an actress, even tried out for a couple of school plays. But when she didn't get the lead, she just quit. If she couldn't be the star, she bolted. While she was a drama queen, Caitlin couldn't act. But if she wanted to see a Banks family member act, she should see this performance, worthy of Tony, Oscar and Emmy.

"Kirk, that's a little harsh," I say, trying to sound very calm. "But I agree with you. Why would anyone care about this Autumn character? She just seems like a human train wreck."

"I disagree, strongly," Gabby says with a confused look on her face as she probably wonders why I'd attack my work, but you'd think she'd understand. After every victory, no matter how well she did, Gabby always puts down her performance, saying 'I suck'. It's good enough for the team, since they usually win, but I suspect not good enough for her dad, who attends most every game.

"But in this story—" Kirk starts.

"This girl has never succeeded at anything. She feels like a failure. Do you have any idea what that's like? To always feel like you're a loser and letting people down? Do you have—"

"This isn't about me," Kirk snaps. "It's about the girl in this story and I think—"

"You're not talking about a story. You're talking about a person," Gabby fires back.

"Are you saying this girl is real? How would—" he starts.

"She is to me. Have you no feeling for people who make mistakes?"

The room goes silent. Kirk's not used to having his opinions, as loud and as wrong as they are, challenged. Like most bullies, brain or brawn, he doesn't want a fair fight in public.

"People, let's not argue," Dr. Draper says. "It is okay to disagree, but let's keep it respectful. This isn't about anyone's feelings, but instead trying to make you all better writers."

"It is personal to me," Gabby says, trying to avoid eye contact. "I care about this girl. How could you read this story and not care about her as she struggles to do the right thing?"

"I know what's been read here," he says, sounding embarrassed. He's trying to back down, but Gabby's got a full court press all over his ass. "And I don't like the story or the girl."

"How can you say that?" Gabby says. "Are you writing anything? Is anyone reading what you wrote? It must be nice to sit in judgment of others all the time."

"If you understood literature, you'd agree with what I'm saying. Right, Dr. Draper?" he asks. Dr. Draper says nothing. "This is serious stuff, not like shooting a ball in a hoop."

Gabby bolts from her chair and gets in Kirk's face like he's a ref who made a bad call. "How dare you say that! Because I'm an athlete, I can't know anything else? Or is it 'cos I'm black?"

"No, that's not it," Kirk says. He sounds like he's ready to cry.

"I agree, that's not it," I offer. "Kirk's not a racist. He's just an asshole."

"Okay, we're done for today!" Dr. Draper shouts. "Please grab the prompts and everyone's submitted pieces on the way out. Carson, could you please stay?"

Her request elicits the classic 'in trouble' sound as people exit. Gabby turns around to look at me, and I want to mouth 'I love you', but the words, unlike me the other night on the phone, won't come. The new year is two weeks away and I've just made three resolutions. I will tell Gabby I love her, we will do the act to prove that, and I will bring Caitlin home.

"You can't insult Kirk," Dr. Draper says, then motions me to sit at a desk next to her.

"I was just defending Gabby."

"She was doing fine defending herself. You were being defensive about your writing."

"I guess," I mumble.

"Look, after today, I'm doing away with blind readings," she says. "It's not working."

"I agree."

"People are afraid to submit things because they're afraid people will more easily tear it apart. The process is supposed to make things more open, and it's always worked, except..."

"Except?"

"Except I used it with college students, not high-school ones," she says, then sighs. "I'll just let people read aloud and talk directly to the writer. That seems to work with Josh."

I laugh.

"What's so funny?" she asks.

"It works with Josh because the girls—and Kirk—adore him," I tell her, amazed that she's blind to the Sun God. "His writing is really good, but it's the coyness and cuteness of Josh they worship, not just his words."

"I don't know if I agree with that, but I think we'll let people read their own work from now on," Dr. Draper says. "Will you continue to submit these stories?"

"It's a novel," I tell her. "The stories are going to be a novel."

"Carson, that's very ambitious." I can't detect from her tone if she believes I'm up to it.

"If Josh can write a novel, then so can I." I cross my arms and make up my mind.

"Maybe the two of you should work together," she says, showing that you can be smart with advanced degrees like her, yet still be a total idiot. "Most everyone else is writing poetry. Talk with him about it. You might help each other."

"I'll think about it," I say to appease her, but there's no way in hell that's ever happening. The only word I want to say to Josh is 'goodbye' at graduation.

"Carson, you need to learn to take criticism, even if it is not constructive."

"But from Kirk?" I ask. "What gives him the right?"

"Because he's the reader. Once it leaves your hands, it is the reader's story, not yours."

"But why does he have to be so critical?" Words come from my thick head about my thin skin. You'd think with Charlotte then Thien I'd be used to rejection, but no.

She shakes her head. "Because that's what people do. Carson, you have the potential to be a great writer, but if you can't take criticism, you may not have the temperament for it."

"I have a temper and a fondness for mints," I cut.

"And bad puns, it seems."

"Is there any other kind?" She kind of smiles, but I'm guessing she's faking it. I gather my stuff so I can have a few minutes with Gabby before her game.

"You should think about working with Josh," she says as she picks up her briefcase. "Just between us, Carson, you two are the most talented and mature writers in this group."

I drop my book bag on the floor with a loud thud. "Who is better?"

"What?" she asks, like she didn't hear. I can tell from her eyes, she did.

"I asked you who is a better writer, me or Josh Brown?" As she goes mute and avoids eye contact, I have my answer. I let her twist in the wind as I walk toward the hall, but I'm not thinking about the halls of Fenton High, instead the walls in my house. Carol's filled with trophies, certificates and achievements while Caitlin's wall is barren of accomplishment. Anyone like Kirk, who couldn't care less about Autumn, never tasted spicy red anger and sour green envy.

* * * *

Even Gabby's kisses taste bittersweet when we rendezvous later in Mom's Malibu for a few minutes together. "Thanks for saying those things," I tell her.

"You know I play tough defense," she cracks. "Anybody gets in my zone, they get hurt."

"Tell me about it," I say as I reach out to lift up her shirt. She slaps my hand, playfully.

"After the game," she jokes back. "I need all my energy and focus."

"Can I ask you something?" Gabby nods, then rests her head against me as I ask, "Do you think Autumn seems real?"

"She's very real to me," Gabby says. "I guess that's why I care about her so much."

"Dr. Draper wants us to read our own writing from now on. I'm not sure I can do it."

"I'll be there to set a screen for you, Carson," she says and she burrows in deeper.

"I'm not sure how to make other people care about her."

"Why do you care about her?" she asks. I pull her a little tighter. I know I can't half-lie myself out of this anymore. Both my body and brain tell me to put my lips to work on Gabby's mouth rather than speaking words I should've told her a long time ago, but the heart trumps all.

"Because she is real," I confess. Gabby's head lifts from me. "It's my older sister."

Mixed emotions wash over her face. "Are you the character named August in the story?"

"Yea, it's my middle name. Pretty lame, I know."

"How is she?" Gabby asks. When I pause, she grabs my hands and holds them tight. "And, Carson Banks, don't you dare tell me you don't know and I just have to read the rest of the story. If you say that, so help me God, I will drop you like a bad habit."

"I don't know. She just left Christmas morning three years ago."

"Do you know where she is?"

I deflect the question. "After she left, my parents hired a detective. Then Dad lost his job and they couldn't pay anymore, not that he ever found out anything anyway."

"Carson, I'm sorry." She kisses me softly.

"I think if I write her story, maybe I'll learn something," I say. "If I can figure out why she left, maybe I can figure out what it would take to get her to come home."

"Well, remember what I said that first night?" she whispers.

"That her story needed a happy ending?"

"You're the writer. You can write a happy ending for me, can't you?"

"In fiction, yes. In Caitlin… That's her real name. In Caitlin's life, I don't know."

Gabby kisses me again and I know I can't let her down. My quest is about her now, too.

Chapter Twenty-One

Saturday, December 25th
Christmas evening

"How was your flight?" Carol asks when she meets me near the San Diego Airport baggage claim. It's December. She's wearing a red BU T-shirt. I have on my thick gray hoodie.

"Long," I say, but what I'm thinking is I totally understand now why Caitlin always talked about wanting only to travel in First Class. But I don't want to mention Caitlin, yet.

"I'll tell Mom you're here." She sends a quick text. "Now, let's get your luggage."

"You're looking at it," I say, pointing to the one overstuffed book bag.

"Traveling light. That's a good habit for college next year. Where are you going?" she asks as we walk toward the parking lot. The airport is packed with taxis, tourists and too many people.

"I don't know yet, I applied to five schools in Michigan."

"Let me guess, Michigan Tech, Kettering and three other places Dad suggested."

"Sorta," I say, feeling ashamed I didn't take a more active role in selecting the colleges, but it seems like such a waste. Even with financial aid, there's no way I'm going away to school. At best, I'll stay home and go to a college in Flint, like Baker, Mott or U of M-Flint. Tim's been accepted early to MIT. He's going out there over spring break to check it out.

"Where else?" she asks. I shrug, but she's not buying it. "'Fess up. I know Michigan Tech isn't your dream school. Harvard? Yale? University of Hawaii?"

"Princeton," I mumble, as if to hide the sheer absurdity of it.

"Princeton!" she shouts, trying not to laugh. "Whose dream school is in New Jersey?"

"My friend Tim might go there," I lie yet again. I don't tell her the main reason I applied. It's where a dreamy Midwestern boy named F. Scott Fitzgerald attended for a few years.

"Why not Boston College?" She beeps the locks on a new looking Chevy coupe.

"I don't think so," I say, so calmly, but I understand Caitlin's rage. *Why not BC? Because that's where you went, Carol, and there's no way I could do better in school than you. I'm a solid B student, who could do better if I focused more on school and less on watching sports, writing stories and surfing porn.* Carol got As in everything. While my parents never threw that in my face or Caitlin's, Carol's success, and thus our failures, weighed on us both.

"We'll figure it out," she says as we climb in. "Your big sister is on the case now."

"Most applications are due in January, so I better figure it out fast," I say. I haven't a clue about next September, I just need to get through this coming Tuesday when I'll see Caitlin.

"What do you want to do over the next few days?" Carol asks, but I get the feeling she's doing so to be polite. She's talking to me, but her phone seems to be the center of her attention.

"You're working Monday and Tuesday, right?"

"My boss allowed me the two days off," Carol says. "We can go to the beach or —"

"Carol, on Tuesday, I'd really just like to borrow your car and drive around."

"The freeways in San Diego are nothing like back in Michigan."

"I'll be careful. I'm a good driver, no accidents," I say, trying to sound confident.

"I just thought you'd want to spend the time together, that's all," she says, even while looking at her phone and not me. I think of telling her what I realized on the plane. We never spent time together. With six years between us, there wasn't much opportunity. By the time I could've spent time with her, she was in high school setting records for most activities. Carol is family, and as we're talking, I realize I don't know her, and wonder if I should even try. It wasn't just Carol's actions that made Caitlin feel like a failure. It was her attitude. Whenever Caitlin failed, which she did at most things, Carol never comforted or supported her little sister.

"I'm pretty boring," I say, trying to joke my way out as we exit the parking lot. "Maybe it's an independence thing I don't get at home with Mom hovering and Dad expecting failure."

"Well, that wasn't an issue with me, more with our sister," Carol says. I love her, but if she's gonna have this attitude for three days, I'm not sure I'm gonna like her. Maybe because Carol's life always seemed so easy, she can't understand how hard life can be for others.

"Still, it would be important for you to trust me and just let me pretend for one day that I'm actually an independent, mature person? You know, like Mom and Dad always treated you?"

"Okay, let me think about it," she says, but I wonder when she has time to think in between phone checks. As we roar out into traffic, I know two things—she'll cave in, and I'll never see Caitlin because I'll kill myself on these roads. But if I don't, then I know where these roads will take me. Tucked away in my pocket is the MapQuest to the Excalibur Gentlemen's Club near LAX.

* * * *

After dinner, Carol and I sit on the tiny back balcony of her apartment. It overlooks the parking lot of a strip mall. She drinks expensive looking bottled water. I slurp down Dew.

"Carol, tomorrow do you think we could drive up to LA?" I need to get the lay of the land.

"Really?" She snaps yet another photo. Carol is a clicking machine.

"Does that sound odd?" She shows me the photo in case I don't know what I look like.

"No, it just sounds more like something your other sister would have wanted to do, rather than you, Carson," she says. There's no emotion in her voice whatsoever when she says that strange phrase. Other sister. "That girl always had stars in her eyes."

"It just seemed like a fun thing to do. See the sights."

"I was actually worried about taking this job out here because of her. Did you know that?" she asks. "Every time I'd come home from college, that's all she would talk about. Don't you remember? Everything with her was about Brad, Angelina, every *American Idol* or MTV reality show star. She was always talking about trying out for reality TV shows. Her life was a reality TV show!" Carol says. "As someone who watched it, it wasn't a fun show. Not at all."

"Maybe not," I answer. I wish she'd go back to tweeting or whatever instead of this rant.

"My God, if that girl knew I lived this close to LA, she'd have been pounding on the door every day asking me to take her to clubs and parties so she could maybe run into some celebrity. She never figured out that meeting somebody famous doesn't make you famous."

"Do you think about Caitlin much?"

"No, but maybe because of you being here, I'm talking about her."

"Talking about Caitlin," I say the name she's avoiding. "You do remember her name?"

"Carson, of course I remember her name," she mumbles. "Do you think about her a lot?"

"Every single day."

"Well, she didn't hate and resent you like she did me," she says. "And for what? For being successful? For getting good grades? For being popular? She could have had all that."

"But you were first," I tell her. "Don't you know how that twisted Caitlin up inside?"

"What are you saying?" She sets the phone down on the table for the first time tonight.

"You're the oldest, so you couldn't know what it was like for her, even for me. Caitlin felt she never could compete with you. That no matter what she did, you'd already done it and done it better than she ever could," I say, realizing that I share some of the same twisted rage.

"That's not my fault. That's her problem," she says. "She could've been popular. She—"

"I'm not blaming. I'm explaining," I interrupt.

She sighs. "How do you know this? Did she try to poison the water for me with you?"

"I heard things she said. I overheard a lot." The audio for a Christmas three years ago clicks on in the background.

"I guess that's easy to do when everybody's yelling." And the phone's back in her hand.

"Well, Mom and Dad don't yell that much anymore," I say.

"That's a relief." I wait for her to ask me to explain that odd statement, but she doesn't. She looks up from her phone long enough to see my pained expression. "What's wrong?"

"You know why they don't yell anymore, right?" I ask.

"Because my train wreck of a sister is no longer destroying their lives? That's a guess."

"That's part of it, but it wasn't all Caitlin's fault." I love my oldest sister, but I'm starting to think Carol isn't only not perfect, she's not even close to it.

"Carson Banks, you don't believe all that drama during her high-school years, but especially senior year, was Mom and Dad's fault?"

"No, it was my fault for distracting them with all my stupid freshman problems," I say. "It was Grandma's fault for getting sick. It was your fault for excelling. It was all of our faults."

"Wow, I don't know if I want to give you my car now," she says, sharper still. "Why are you acting so immature? Why are you taking her side?"

"I'm not taking *her* side, I'm taking Caitlin's side! Can't you even say her name?"

"Caitlin's dead," Carol says without any emotion. My eyes open wide. "Not dead, dead—or maybe she is. I don't know. I don't care. She's gone, out of our lives."

"Not for me." Carol's words add intensity to my quest, if only to prove her wrong.

"You're young, but a lesson you learn in life is how to deal with loss," she says. "I accept that our sister is gone. I don't think about her. You shouldn't either."

Should was once both Mom's and Dad's favorite word. I know that should isn't a word, it's a trap. "How could you *not* think about her? How could you *not* wonder?"

She takes a photo of the sunset and starts clicking away again. "Just let it go."

"But what if? What if I knew, we knew, where she was?"

"No, Carson. It doesn't matter if she's dead or alive. All that matters is she's gone."

As the hot sun sets into the cool of the evening, I ask, "How can you be so cold?"

"That's the thing about loss," Carol says. "You get over it or it will get all over you."

Carol heads back inside, eyes on her phone all the while. I stay on the balcony and try to figure out which way is north, which way is LA. So, I guess all this time

I wasn't writing an epic fantasy about a prince rescuing the damsel in distress. It turns out, according to Carol's thinking, I've been writing a zombie novel. When I get to LA, I wonder… Will I be able to raise the dead?

Chapter Twenty-Two

Tuesday, December 28th
Morning and early afternoon

"You have my work number, right?" Carol says as I drop her off at her office.

"And your work cell and iPhone," I answer. "With traffic, I might be late."

"Call if you're going to be late," she says sharply, sounding a lot like Mom. I finally got the car from Carol by telling her by not trusting me with it she was acting like Mom. "If so, I'll get a ride home, but you shouldn't be out driving on these highways late at night. Be careful."

"I will." She looks worried. She should be. She gets off work at six in San Diego. Caitlin goes on stage at four in LA.

"And don't wreck my car," she says, now sounding like Dad.

Sadly, given our interaction—or lack thereof over the past two days—I think she's more worried about her stuff than me. We didn't have a meal without frantic texting. We didn't drive more than five miles without a call, mostly from her boss. I didn't hear his part, just Carol agreeing to do whatever she was told, acting more like a serf than an honor roll scholar. It seems odd for a fancy phone and new car, but not enough to fly home more than once a year. I thought it was because she thought she was too good for us, but I wonder if it's because she's not good enough. She's no longer the brightest girl in school or the big fish in the small pond. She's just another person working another job. I wonder if the dreams she had have all vanished. While she'll never know it, she's never had more in common with Caitlin than she does right now.

The drive to LA quickly becomes the nightmare I'd imagined. I'm used to people driving fast—everyone in Michigan drives eighty miles an hour, and that's just in the McDonald's drive-through lane. People here can't drive fast—the traffic barely moves—but they drive crazy. Cutting in and out of lanes like this was a video game, not a highway. I'll put on my signal, but the only signal other people seem to use is a horn and a middle finger.

While I don't plan on visiting any LA landmarks, I have time to kill before Caitlin's shift starts at four p.m. for something called 'Gentlemen's Happy Hour'. I'm hoping my parents don't ask Carol about today or she doesn't feel the need to tell them. The only reason all of this has managed to go unnoticed, I can only assume, is that no one could imagine I'd do all of these things. Most of my life I've done everything I was supposed to, so this isn't any different. I'm trying to help a family member out of a bad situation. No matter how many lies I've told to people, no matter how irresponsibly I've acted, it was for good reasons. The end justifies...

By one p.m., I'm in the parking lot, just in case she comes in early, but I can't imagine she would want to set foot in a place like this one second before she needed to. Or wanted to? That's part of what I must understand. Is Caitlin doing this because she needs the money or because she wants the attention, even the sad flicker of stardom that a place like this brings her?

I'm parked so I can see the employee door, which is good. If I saw the customer door, I think I'd want to shout at everyone to stay out. But I don't shout or move. I just wait and watch. Though I've had almost three whole months to imagine the conversation, I have almost no idea what I will actually say to her. Like so many stories I've thought of but never written, all I know is the opening line. After spending time with Carol, I wonder if talking to Caitlin will be like talking to someone who looks like me, shares the same parents, but who I really don't know.

I take out my notebook, click the pen and start jotting notes of things I want to say. It's hard because I'll write for just a few seconds, then go back to staring at the door. Every now and then a car will pass by or park near the customer door. It's usually not a fancy car — a lot like Mom's old Malibu — and some guy, about Dad's age, will slink from the car. With the windows rolled down, I can almost smell their sweat of desperation and sadness. Caitlin might be working the 'Gentlemen's Happy Hour', but I doubt these guys are gentlemen — or very happy.

I'm glad I know nobody here since I'm embarrassed that somebody might drive by and think I'm the kind of guy who goes to these places. Only, of course, that's exactly the kind of guy I am. Would things have worked out differently for me if I'd never visited a porn site in my life? Would I not have made that terrible mistake with Thien? There's one thing I do know. If I didn't visit sites like that—me and a couple million other males—there'd be no places like this. In Flint, they talk about busting gang-banger drug dealers. If there were no buyers, there'd be no sellers. Caitlin being here is partially my fault, but not in a way that I imagined.

By two, I'm feeling anxious from all the waiting. The liter of Dew isn't helping. Still with one eye on the door, I call Gabby with the prepaid cell I bought for the trip. The lie is to ask about her first tournament game tonight, but the real reason is I just want to hear her voice.

"Hey, Gabby, it's Carson," I say when she answers.

"How's California?" she asks. "It's snowing here."

"It's like seventy-five, without a cloud in the sky."

"Sweet," she says. "Have you been to the beach yet for me?"

"Not yet."

"You make sure to go. Imagine us walking on the beach at sunset, okay?"

"Okay. Any word yet?" I ask, hesitant. Not only has she heard from no California schools, but even the Michigan colleges Gabby thought might give her an athletic scholarship have yet to contact her with an offer. I watched Mom ask Dad every day for a year if he'd found a job, until he finally exploded at her. "*Don't you think if I found a job I would have told you?*"

"No," she says, as reluctant to answer as I was to ask.

"Maybe there'll be some college recruiters there tonight."

"Maybe, but if so, just Michigan schools," she says. "I want to be there."

"Well, you've worked hard. I'm sure you'll be rewarded."

"Working hard, you should have seen me last night," she says, then starts to tell me about yesterdays' practice. I listen, but I'm distracted. Not by the door, which hasn't had any action in the last half hour, but by Gabby's belief. She believes she'll get a scholarship. I fear she won't and she'll be heartbroken. She believes dreams come true. I know they don't. Dad's life is exhibit A. Caitlin's exhibit XXX.

"Tonight's game is against Carman. Should be hard, but we'll dominate," Gabby says, and I realize I'd better say something before she thinks I'm dead, or asks me where I am.

"Gabby, can I ask you something?"

"How many points I'll score? I'd say double figures most definite," she says.

"There's only one way you'd not score double figures—" I start.

"If I was white," she cracks.

"Hey, Gabby, something serious," I say, and take a deep breath. "You know how you told me that Autumn deserved a second chance? Why?"

"Why I told you Autumn deserved a second chance?" she repeats.

"What do you think it means to give someone a second chance?" I ask.

She pauses. Pauses long enough for me to stare intensely at the employee door. There's some activity.

Two girls, one Asian, one black, just went inside. "Gabby, are you there?"

"Carson, to give someone a second chance means you forgive them for their mistake, even if what they did hurt you really bad or disappointed you. It means you love them no matter what they did, and you make sure the person doesn't make another mistake. A second chance is all most people need if they learn from the mistakes in their life. Do you know what I mean?"

Before I can answer, a blonde, cigarette in hand, emerges from a red Eclipse.

"Gabby, I got to go," I say. "I love you."

I click the phone so fast there's no time for her to respond to the promise I made with those three words. Like when you're writing, sometimes you just react, and reveal the real you.

"Callie!" I shout. She doesn't turn. "Callie! Callie!" Still nothing. "Caitlin!" I yell, and she turns. As I walk toward her, I wonder if she looks and sounds the same as when she left three years ago. Is she Callie now, or is Caitlin still alive?

Chapter Twenty-Three

Tuesday, December 28th
Late afternoon

"Carson?" Caitlin asks, as her bright red lips open, but not as wide as her eyes when she pulls off her sunglasses.

"Caitlin, come home," I say as planned, then I wait. Three years of emotions, three months of anticipation and infinite hope sweep through me as I wait for her to respond.

Caitlin takes a step toward me, but stops short of an awkward hug or answering my plea. I look like a dork in my Mountain Dew T-shirt, standing by a blonde in a short red dress.

"You're alive," I say, stating the obvious. "We missed you so much."

"Maybe you, but certainly not Mom, Dad or Carol," she says, angry as ever.

"Everybody."

She cracks a small smile. "Then why are you standing here alone?"

"Where have you been? What happened that morning when you left home? I heard—"

"Everybody will know that story once I make it big out here. It will be part of the story of the sacrifices I made to become a celebrity," she says.

I don't know if I should laugh or cry.

"We were worried." Just like saying 'I love you' to Gabby falls short of describing the depth of that emotion, worried doesn't capture the abyss of anguish we felt after Caitlin left.

She stares at me, then takes a drag on the cigarette. I want her silence to mean that she has so much to say that she can't decide what to say next. But, there's just smoking. I notice new rose and barbed wire tattoos on her arms, a new nose piercing and plucked thin eyebrows, but behind Callie, I'm looking for Caitlin. "So, you're eighteen, right?" is her odd response.

"Couple of weeks."

"Well, come in the employee entrance. I'll sneak you in."

"I'm not here to see the show," I say firmly.

She stares at me again, or maybe she never stopped. "Then what do you want?"

I break the stare and look at the parking lot. "Like I said, I want you to come home."

Again, the stare, the smoke and the silence.

"Caitlin, I *need* you to come home." I wonder if she notices the important word swap.

She takes a final drag on the cigarette then crushes it under her heel. "No."

"Caitlin, how can you do this?"

"What do you know about it?" she snaps. "I'm happier here than I was at home."

"I don't believe you," I say as those first images I found online haunt me like a ghost.

"You don't know anything about my life," she says. "I need to go to work."

"How can you do this?" Bad music from the club oozes out of the open door.

"It's my job," she says, her volume up. "I see the news. Dad's out of work, right?"

"Yes," I mumble.

"And what career is Mom failing at now?" she asks, but doesn't wait for an answer. "Face it. Our parents are losers. I'm not going to be a loser. I'm going to be a winner. I'm going to be famous. If you don't want to be a loser, then get away from them as soon as you can."

"I'm not a loser," I say. "And neither are Mom and Dad. It's just hard times right now."

"I bet I make more bills than Princess Carol. What's she doing?"

I feel like I'm the middle child, not Caitlin. "She works for a big software company."

"Figures," she mumbles.

I want to say, *While you work for a hardcore company,* but I swallow it. Swallow it because it's not funny, it's not fair, but mostly, it's not time.

"I wonder how it feels for her to be one in a crowd." A smirk lights up Caitlin's heavily made-up face, but it's still familiar. Her life has changed, but her self looks similar.

I hold my tongue. I need to build bridges, not burn them by letting Caitlin know despite her body, her beauty and even her brains, that's she not special at all. She's one of the thousands of girls on computer screens and club stages. To the men who look at her, she's less than one in a crowd, she's not even a person. She's pixels of flesh for their fantasies. "Caitlin, this isn't about Carol, or even Mom and Dad. This is about you coming home."

"Carson, what would I do in Michigan?" I have no answer. "The strip bars there are filled with middle-age losers like Dad. They don't tip and they can't help me get famous."

Now I stare in silence. Had she worked as a stripper in Flint? Is she saying Dad went to strip clubs? Did Dad see her and tell her to get out of town, but didn't tell the rest of us? How could he know she was alive and not tell? What kind of person would do that? Oh, right, me.

"I just know I need to bring you home with me."

"Carson, that's not happening until I become a star." She checks her phone. "I gotta go."

She takes a step away, but I finally touch her, grabbing her tattooed left arm. This isn't at all how I imagined this going down. I would ask her to come home, and she'd agree. That was the scene I wrote, but she's not sticking to the script. "Caitlin, you can't be happy doing this."

"What? I'm a stripper so I can't be happy? I make a lot of people happy, so why would you assume that I'm not happy?" She pulls her left arm away, but then shows both her arms to me. "Look, no track marks. I bet you think all strippers are junkies, don't you?"

"I don't know." Because I don't want to know. Better not to think of them as people.

"I'm not a meth fiend or a pill head like some of these girls. This is none of your business."

"You're my sister. It is my business."

"And this is *my* life. All of you can look down on me like you always did and—"

"Caitlin, I always looked up to you," I say, sounding more like seven than seventeen.

Now she goes silent. The club door opens again and loud music pours out. I don't hear any laughter, or joy, just music masking the desperation of those on stage and those watching.

"Well, maybe you'll look up to me even more when I'm fucking famous," she says.

"Maybe." It clicks like a memory into place—same words, same tone, same Caitlin.

"What, you don't believe in me? Like Mom and Dad, always putting down my dreams," she says, angry hot. "I'm going to make it and you'll all see. This is a detour until I make it big."

"But being up on a stage with all those men watching—" I start.

"Listen, I was the middle child living in the shadow of a perfect person!"

"Carol isn't perfect." After spending two days with her, this is no lie.

"Don't you get it, Carson?" She looks like she wants to jab her fingers into my chest, except the long, fake red nails would probably break on impact. "Carol already filled the role of overachieving daughter, so what choice did I have? She was the all-American dream girl."

"So you took the role of bad girl?"

"Exactly! The family fuck-up," she says, then stops to light up another smoke. She doesn't look at her ringing phone, and she ignores the two girls, one redhead, one brunette, who walk past her. They say hello, but she waves them off.

My tone turns begging as I say, "Mom and Dad would understand. You could still—"

"They never understood me, never understood a thing about me," she says. "They never took time—Dad always working or going to school, Mom working or taking care of Grandma. Face it, Carson. They just didn't love me like they did you and Carol. That's not your fault."

"I don't know how they felt, so let me tell you how I feel. Just three little words. I love you."

"I know," she says. "I always loved you, Carson. I never meant to hurt you in all this."

"I don't know what else to say," I confess. "Everything you say is probably true. I don't know. I just know this. I need you to come home. This is your second chance."

She laughs. "I think I used up all my second chances."

Mom's and Dad's words echo in my ears.

"Caitlin. Come home." I step forward. She moves her smoke aside and lets me hug her.

"I can't," she whispers, and I hold her tight. "I have to go to work."

She returns the hug, then takes a step back. She reaches into her purse, puts on more bright red lipstick, then checks her phone again. She's leaving. I've flown all this way and accomplished nothing. I tried being understanding, but I can't stand avoiding the truth.

"You do more than strip. You're doing porn." My voice trembles as much as my hand.

She turns around and stares at me like she did when I first saw her. It's like we hit Replay on the machine, only this time, I'm going to tell her everything I know. No holding back, but I will hold her. I grab her left wrist and latch on, then describe to her in detail only a few of the photos and videos of her I've seen. I don't let go until there are tears. My tears, not hers.

"Don't judge me," she says slowly, like each word was a sentence.

"I'm not judging you. I'm releasing you," I say, even if the right word is rescue. "My plane leaves tomorrow. When Mom and Dad find out that you're coming home, they'll—"

"So they don't know about you being here?" she says. "About me? About this?"

"No, nobody knows about this," I say, looking at the gray asphalt in front of me. "I kept it a secret."

"Thanks, but I'm not ashamed of who I am or what I do," she says defiantly.

"But I am," I confess. She stares at me one more time, then turns to walk away.

"I'm sorry I'm such a family embarrassment. It's good I'm away from you," she says. "I have to get back to work. This is my life now. There's nothing you can say to change that."

"Can you answer a question??" My voice trembles like a small LA earthquake.

Her hands go on her hips, hips she'll be shaking on stage in an hour. "What?"

"What happened Christmas morning with the gun?"

A stare like fire burns a hole in my heart. Silence like ice spikes my skull. She flips her shades down. I can't see if she's crying. I stare at her eyes, but the sunglasses act like mirrors. I can't see her eyes. I just see mine, filled with tears and glistening in the hot, bright California sun on the second darkest day of my life.

Chapter Twenty-Four

Friday, December 31st
New Year's Eve

"Are you feeling okay?" the flight attendant asks me moments after I've climbed on the flight from San Diego back to Detroit on Wednesday morning. She would have had to have been blind not to have seen my red eyes or deaf not to hear my sniffing. I didn't wish I was okay or not okay. I wished I wasn't feeling anything.

"Do you want a glass of water?"

"I'm fine," I lie. If the water could be filled with fifty sleeping pills, then maybe.

"If you need anything, you push the button here," she says, pointing above me. Wow, if life were only that easy. You push a button and help comes running. But, as I learned with Caitlin, there's no sense coming to someone's rescue if they won't admit they need saving.

"My sister died," I mumble. It seems the only two kinds of people in the world you can be totally honest with are perfect strangers—why should they care?—and your most perfect friends—because they care so much. It's the in-betweens you need to watch for. As the flight attendant struggles with what to say, I think about Gabby, her perfection and my secrets.

"I'm so sorry," the woman says, but then stops because there's nothing anyone can say after those three big words that makes one damn bit of difference. "Let me get you that water."

"Thanks," I say, but by the time she gets back, I've clicked my pen and started writing the next chapter in Autumn's story. When the wheels of the plane touch down at Detroit Metro some three hours later, Autumn's story, like Caitlin's connection to me, feels finished. I'm sad, and Gabby's going to be mad at me for the lack of a happy ending.

* * * *

I claimed jet lag the moment I got into the car with my folks at Metro Airport as an excuse not to talk. I'd been so busy writing not-so-fictional fiction on the plane that I'd forgotten the lies I told Carol about where I spent the last day of my trip, just in case she and my parents had compared notes. The hardest part about lying so often isn't morality, but memory.

By tonight, my parents and I have moved on to other topics unrelated to my trip to California, more related to my New Year's outing. Normally I use the cover story of attending a game for the newspaper to meet up with Gabby, but that won't fly tonight. I tell them I'm helping Tim at work. I doubt they'll check on that story, but if so, as my best friend, Tim understands lying for me is part of the friend job description.

"We want you home by eleven p.m.," Dad reminds me for the eleventh time.

"Sure, and guess what, I'll even drive carefully," I remind them for the twelfth time. I don't know if they'd be shocked or proud to know I safely navigated California expressways.

"Just be safe," Mom says, and I try not to laugh as I wonder if somehow she developed super powers, like X-ray vision. Be safe? Did they find the Trojans stashed in my bedside bureau? Mom, I want to say, I'm thinking the exact the same thing.

* * * *

"So how long is your dad gone tonight?" I ask Gabby when I climb into her car. Per usual, I've parked at McDonald's on Owens Road, and she picked me up.

"This is a busy night for him," she says, sounding distracted. She doesn't ask about the bag from the San Diego airport gift shop I smuggled out of my house and now hold in my hand.

"Your dad has an important job," I say. "When people get in trouble, he helps them out."

She laughs. "Carson, he's a tow truck driver, not a doctor like Josh's parents."

"Maybe, but after an accident, next to the ambulance, he's the guy you want to see."

"Not always," she says, and I give her a strange look. "What do you mean?"

"It's not all rescues. These days, he's doing a lot of repo work," she says. "He's making good money, but it must be hard to do that by towing away some guy's dream car."

"In that case, my parents and he will meet one day after all," I say, half joking, half sad.

Gabby changes the subject, so we talk about school and sports, filled with sexual innuendo, on the way to her house. She pulls the SUV into the garage and we exit quickly. She calls her dad, asking questions to determine that he won't be returning to the house any time soon. She ends the conversation saying, "Okay, I won't wait up." She clicks the phone, smiles broadly, and we melt into each other on the sofa. After a while, we come up for air.

"I got you a belated Christmas gift," I say, pointing to the bag sitting on the floor.

"Carson, you didn't need to do that."

"Sorry, I didn't have time to wrap it," I say, and force back a laugh. "Open it."

She opens the bag and pulls out four jerseys from southern California schools — USC, UCLA, Long Beach and San Diego State. The little money my parents gave me for my trip went on her gifts. "Next fall, one of those schools will be graced by The Great Gabby's presence. Get it, presence, presents?" She rolls her big browns, but can't quit smiling. "Carson, I didn't—"

I cut her off. "It's not too late for a gift. Why don't you try them on?"

Gabby gives me a skeptical look, then an exaggerated sigh. "Carson Banks, what am I going to do with you?" she says as she pulls the Detroit Pistons T-shirt over her head.

"Well, I have a suggestion," I say. "Why don't we play shirts and skins? I'll be shirts."

She doesn't say anything. I hear the tiny clicking sound as she unhooks her bra. Gabby never gets to trying on the shirts. After a while, I say, "Gabby, let's move into the other room."

"The kitchen?" she says sarcastically. "The dining room?"

"Well, I'm hungry for you," I say, then whisper dirty details into her ear. She pushes me back. "Slow down." Man, she plays mean D off the court, too.

"Gabby, it's time," I say gently. In porn, that time is twenty seconds after two people meet.

"I'm not ready, Carson." She puts on the bright white and gold USC shirt. "Are you mad?"

"No, Gabby, I'm not mad," I say. "I'm frushappanger."

"What?" I explain my made-up word for frustration, happiness and anger.

"I'm just disappointed," I add.

"Carson, look, I can't have sex with you."

"I don't like that 'with you' part. Would you say that with someone else?" I wonder aloud.

"There is nobody else," she says, firmly. "I just can't."

"Won't," I say just as firmly.

"What?"

"Can't implies that you don't have a choice. Turning iron into gold is something people can't do. It is physically impossible. Won't means you can, but choose not to."

"Thanks for the grammar lesson," she snaps. "Fine. Won't. Is that a problem?"

"What do you think?" I ask as I fall into that dark void that separates my dreams from my daily life. I narrow my eyes as I slip into that deep crevice, while hers grow wider with her anger.

"You should respect my decision," she says harshly. "If you can't, then maybe we—"

"Wait, foul for overreaction!" I make the ref technical foul signal. "This isn't a fuck me or fuck you ultimatum. I want to be with you, Gabby, that's all. I'll take as much of you as you can give me."

"And that's a lot, because," she starts, then points from her head to her toes.

"I'm tall, for a girl," we say together. The shared laugher breaks the tension.

I know this is my chance, so I whisper, "Look, the Valentine's Day dance is coming up."

"No, I can't do that," she says, sounding angry.

"Does your dad hang around school?" Anger serve returned. "He won't find out."

She sighs. "You know how high school is. Someone tells someone who tells someone."

"None of this other stuff matters. What matters is I love you."

More silence, waiting for the 'I love you' return, but there's only the sound of our lips. I touch the not-to-be-used condom in my pocket. If sex can be safe, then why can't love?

C h a p t e r   T w e n t y - F i v e

Sunday, January 9th
Carson's birthday

"What time?" Tim asks. He's still not used to talking on the phone, instead of IMing. For the most part I kept another New Year's resolution, staying away from porn. Sadly, the only way to do that has been to stay off the computer. I'm such an all-or-nothing kind of guy.

"What time for what?" I ask.

"It's your eighteenth birthday, dude. Don't you remember?" he asks.

"Tim, maybe I'm having a senior — get it, senior? — moment," I crack.

"You said on your eighteenth birthday that we'd go to a strip club on Dort Highway."

"Tim, I'm sorry. I wasn't serious."

There's a long pause. "Tim, you still there?"

"I thought we'd hang out, that's all," he says, backtracking. I'm relieved I don't need to explain to

Tim my lack of interest in strippers or being around people who watch strippers.

"Dude, I'd love to, but I'm low-keying it," I say. "I'm having dinner with my parents, and then me and Dad are just going to watch some of the football play-offs. Nothing special."

"No prob." Other than the truth, the biggest casualty in Gabby's and my relationship is Tim. All he knows is Gabby and I are spending time and keeping it a secret.

"Look, next week, we'll cut school and hit that Indian buffet for lunch," I say.

"Which one?" The Flint area is a buffet of buffets. As my dad always says, the food isn't good, but there's a lot of it.

"The trough Mahal," I joke. We crack up, as if on cue.

"You had me at buffet," Tim jokes back. We're laughing stupidly, like we're high.

"Or maybe you'd prefer to eat Vietnamese," I say. "Any action in the Thien arena?"

"You are so immature."

I don't deny it, even on my eighteenth birthday.

"And you, Tiny Tim Wang, are still my best friend."

"Well, if that's the case, then maybe we could hang out more."

"As I was saying," I say, then clear my throat for effect. "Anything with Thien?"

"I've known her for so long. It's hard for me to think of her in that way."

"In that way! What? Are you in junior high?"

"Sexually, yes," he replies. "But I suspect there'll be one big problem."

"What's that?" I ask, but I know. He pauses. It's a vocal pistol. The handle's cocked.

"Carson, I can tell that she really hates you."

"Sorry, dude." He doesn't ask why, so the bullet only grazes me, this time.

"So I don't know what to do," he says, then waits for me to answer. Ten, maybe twenty seconds go by without my responding, because I have no idea what to say or do.

"Why don't you come over, pick up some food? Dinner is on me," he finally says.

"The image of dinner on you makes me never want to eat again," I joke. Later, I'll place an order to go. For now, I couldn't order a better friend than Tim. I hope the meal contains a fortune cookie with answers to this latest, but I'm sure not last, dilemma of my senior year.

* * * *

After finishing too many boxes of Chinese food, Dad and I go into the living room to watch football. It's the only TV left. They've sold all the rest. If Caitlin were to come home, I don't think she'd recognize the house. The plasma TVs and other electronic toys that once filled the Banks household are gone. The play-off game isn't that good, but it's fun because Dad and I provide better commentary than the guys on NBC. During half-time, I sneak out to call Gabby.

"Sorry we couldn't get together," I say.

"I wish you could come over," she says.

I go mum as an image of Gabby in ecstasy overwhelms me.

"You still there?" she asks.

"Just thinking about you in your birthday suit."

"Really? That again? Carson, you have a one-track mind," she says, then sighs.

"On that one track is the Gabby train, and, baby, you've got a nice caboose."

"Carson, you're killing me. You know flattery will get you most everywhere."

"It's okay. I notice I have one of these birthdays every year on the exact same day."

"I wish I could be there with you," she almost purrs.

"Maybe I could pretend you are," I say, which prompts another round of phone sex.

After cleaning up and catching my breath, I say, "Josh doesn't know how lucky he is."

"Carson, what are you talking about?" she replies to my odd remark.

"If you wrote like you just talked," I say, "you'd blow his ass out of the water."

"The very water he walks on," she adds.

"Gabby, maybe next time we talk like this, you could be the one who—" I start.

But she cuts me off. "Carson, I have to go."

"I hate to see you go," I whisper. "But I'd love to see you come."

* * * *

I'm no more than a few minutes watching the game, when the phone rings. It's the landline—one in the kitchen, one in my room. Gabby only calls when she knows I'm home, so I expect the phone is her calling back. But before I can get to the phone, the ringing stops.

"Who was it?" Dad yells across the house. Mom's in the kitchen doing something.

"They hung up," she yells back.

I settle back to watch the game, when the phone rings again. This time, I give a loud "I got it" shout. I race into the kitchen and pick up the phone. I'm out of breath. "Hey."

There's silence. Maybe Gabby's just enjoying my heavy breathing. Again.

"Hello?" I say into the silence.

"Happy birthday, Carson."

I put my hand over the receiver, then whisper, "Caitlin?" Mom doesn't react.

"You see, I remembered," she says. "I just wanted to wish you a happy birthday."

"Wait. Please, talk with me."

She coughs, then asks, "So, did Carol call yet?"

"No, she sent a message on Facebook."

"Remember which of your sisters called you."

"What about calling Dad on his birthday? It's March 15th. Or maybe call on Easter Sunday. Remember when we all used to get dressed up and get pictures taken with—"

"No, Carson, I'm calling you today. I'm talking to *you*," she says. "You're the only one there who gives a shit about me. I always knew that, but your trip out here proved that to me."

I pause. Talking with Caitlin is like a game of chess, which I used to play with Tim, who beat me every time. I need to think of what to say three moves ahead to keep her connected.

"I got those three words for you," she says when it seems I've forgotten how to talk.

"What's that?" I ask, remembering her last three words to me and the last said in this house.

"I love you," she says, then hangs up the phone. She may have hung up, but she's reaching out, letting me know she's still alive. That means there's still a chance — maybe.

I excuse myself from Dad and head upstairs to my Mac. On the screen, my story stares at me. As I make small revisions, I wish I could erase the final moments of Caitlin's life in this house from my memory, but instead I tell the truth through fiction in the next chapter of *Autumn's Fall*.

Chapter Twenty-Six

Excerpt from Autumn's Fall
'Christmas Climax – or Christmas Cataclysm?'

"Who's there?" August's mom yelled at the front door from the kitchen.

"Get that! We're busy," his Dad yelled back, way too loud. Maybe it was the pressure of the holidays or worrying about Autumn, but August could tell his dad was cracking. His father would never admit to it, but the eight empty beer bottles from last night told a different story.

"Fine, fine," his mom said, her tone that of someone pretending to be happy as opposed to someone who was happy. Autumn's disappearance on Thanksgiving had left more sadness than anger in their home. She'd been seen around town, but not school or their house. She wouldn't even return my phone calls.

"It's Autumn!" his mom shouted as she opened the door. August's dad got the strangest looks on his face, like some sort of emotional Wheel of Fortune. But when his dad slammed his fist onto the floor, August knew the wheel had landed on red anger.

"What do you want?" August's dad yelled, while August rushed toward the door.

"We were so worried." August's mom opened her arms, but Autumn's arms remained folded across her chest. Although she'd left a month ago with one suitcase, when she took off her coat, August saw she was dressed not like a runaway, but like a model on the runway, like somebody with access to a credit card — their dying-of-cancer grandmother's credit card. August had found an overdue bill on another card. She lied, he snitched and hated himself.

Autumn stared at August, like she wanted him to say something, but no words came. Amber spoke instead. "What's today's melodrama performance, Autumn?"

Autumn didn't respond. She just kept staring at August. Only her eyes spoke. They said, Help me, please. But August turned his back on his family's prodigal problem middle child.

"Amber, August, please go up to your rooms," their dad said.

"Daddy, I'm not fourteen. You can't—" Amber started.

"Now!" he shouted, and Amber did as she'd always done — obeyed. She and August walked upstairs without a word. He watched Amber go into her room, but August merely opened then closed the door to his. Instead, he lay on the floor near the edge of the stairs.

"If you want to stay here, you're going to do things our way," he heard his dad yell.

Autumn spoke, but August couldn't hear it.

"We were so worried about you," August's mom said. "We don't know—"

"I'm not perfect like Amber. I'm just a fuck-up!" Autumn shouted. August couldn't make out the rest of her words, but it didn't matter. This wasn't about words. If words solved every problem, then August would be ecstatic all day. So would his dad with his crossword puzzles. But life wasn't a series of little black and white squares with clues.

"No one is asking you to be perfect," his mom said.

"Good, then I don't need to change my name to Amber," Autumn replied.

"Stop that," his dad said. "I'm so tired of that. Stop blaming everyone but yourself."

"Then whose fault is it?" Autumn fired back. "I know for sure it's not yours!"

"It's your fault, Autumn," Dad said. Loud. Firm. Final.

"Big surprise," Autumn replied.

"Honey, you can't change unless you admit you're wrong," her mom added.

"Stop your therapist crap on me," Autumn said. "Lot a good that did you two, right?"

"This isn't about your mother or me, but you," Autumn's father said.

"It should be!" Autumn shouted. "Daddy, maybe if you'd sober up and fuck her every now and then, she wouldn't need therapy." A hard slap from one of their parents silenced her.

"You hateful, ungrateful child!" her mom shouted. "Leave this house right now!"

"Tossing your daughter out on Christmas," Autumn said. "Really Christian of you."

"You threw yourself out," his dad replied. "Your actions, your consequences."

"I messed up. I want a second chance," Autumn fired back. "I know it's hard with a perfect daughter like Amber, but people make mistakes. I said I'm sorry. What do you want?"

August heard his mother sigh loudly. "Lord knows where you stayed these past weeks!"

"I fucked for my rent," Autumn said. "You got me to say it. Are you happy? Are —"

Autumn's words again get slapped from her mouth. Silence returned until August's mom said through tears, "You stole from my dying mother. How could you do this? Who are you?"

"I can't live like this anymore," his dad said, his words fading, followed by footsteps.

"Daddy, where are you going?" Autumn shouted. More steps, a door opened, then closed.

"Autumn, we ground you, you ignore it," August's mom said. "We show we love you, and you look at us with such hate. I don't know what else we can do."

Autumn mumbled something in return. August hoped it was a family-saving apology.

"If we can't love you or control you, then we can't have you live here," his mom said.

There was silence, except for maybe crying. August wasn't sure this time who was crying until her heard his mom say, "Autumn, honey. Please don't cry." August inched closer.

"I'm so sorry, so sorry for everything," Autumn wailed. "I want a second chance."

"You've used up your second chances," August's mom said. "There are some things you can't forget or forgive even if —"

But her words were cut short by the sound of the door opening then heavy footsteps headed back into the living room. August moved closer, risking being seen, but he wanted to hear everything. He expected his dad to say something, but there were just shouts from the women.

"Oh my God, no," his mom yelled. "What in God's name are you thinking?"

"Daddy, what are you doing?" Autumn shouted.

"Autumn, here's a pistol. Take it from me," August's dad said. "Either kill yourself or kill us. We can't live with what you've done and what you've become. Take it and end this!"

August heard nothing for ten seconds

Nothing except the beating of his heart.

Then twenty seconds.

Nothing except his mind overheating with worry.

Then thirty seconds.

The silence of a life-and-death decision was the loudest sound in the universe.

August started downstairs to protect his family, but was stopped before he reached the bottom of the stairs. He wasn't stopped by a loud gunshot, but by the metallic clicking sound caused by the trigger against an empty chamber. He could only hear the click, not see the faces. Who pulled the trigger? Where was the gun pointed?

In the distance, he heard Autumn shout, "I hate you!" followed by the clicking of her high heels across the floor then a final click — the door closing as Autumn left their life forever.

Chapter Twenty-Seven

Thursday, January 20th
Creative writing club meeting

"Does everybody understand?" Dr. Draper asks the increasingly smaller number of us attending creative writing club. Gabby's not here due to an away basketball game. It's down to Kirk, Josh, Charlotte, Candy, three of the roses and razor blade freshman girl poets and me.

Before anybody has a chance to confirm with her that we understand we'll now be reading our own works, Josh jumps right in with his latest opus called 'Tenderness on the Block'. It's the story of a smart, sensitive-type boy who loves palindromes. While palindromes are perfectly balanced words, the MC can't seem to find his perfect girl. The story involves a SSB — smart, sensitive-type boy — and his smart-mouth cousin — the wacky sidekick, aka WSK — who both fall in love with same beautiful, mysterious girl, or BMG.

As with all of Josh's stories for the paper and in this club, it is well written and universally adored. Even though I can think of some constructive things to say, I don't bother. With him and Charlotte, no matter what I'd say, it would smell, taste and sound like sour grapes.

I pretend to listen as one of the emo girls pours out her agony stanzas like she's the first person ever to feel pain. My head hurts under the deluge of abstract nouns gushing from her black lipsticked mouth. When there's very little time left in the meeting, I finally raise my hand.

"Carson, you have a short story to read?" Dr. Draper asks.

"This is the last *Autumn's Fall* story." I open up the folder I'm clutching in my shaking right hand. "All these stories are connected, really more of a novel than a collection of stories."

"That's an excellent idea," she says. "So you're submitting all four we've seen?"

"Maybe," I answer. "The new one is too long to read aloud."

Josh doesn't react to my subtle shot, nor does he take one of my stories. Charlotte grabs one, however, then quickly scans it before she says, "I knew it. I knew these were your stories."

"How?"

"Because they're so good," she says. Josh doesn't react. That would be beneath him.

"I wouldn't go that far," Kirk says.

"That's not helpful," Dr. Draper says. "If you have comments to make Carson's story better, fine, but don't just snipe. That's as bad as writing a review and not signing your name."

"I just think it's all too emotional," Kirk continues. "Nobody would care about a girl like this. She's a slut, a liar and a substance abuser. She deserves a jail term, not our sympathy."

"Kirk, what you don't know about the world is a lot," I tell him.

"The good thing about Carson's story," Dr. Draper interjects, "is that he made some of you care about this character. I remember Miss Gibson being quite taken with your story."

"Well, that's because it uses mostly little words," Kirk cracks. Nobody laughs except him. The razor blade girls are too busy swooning over Josh and resenting Charlotte.

"Just like not all critics and editors are failed writers," I crack back as I point to Kirk.

"Real funny, Banks. Maybe you should spend more time writing your stories for the paper than writing jokes." He's got me. I'm covering Gabby with more kisses than ink.

"We're here to talk about writing, not launch into personal attacks," Dr. Draper says.

"But if you attack my writing, you're attacking me," I say.

"No, that's what you don't get, Carson," Kirk says, up in my face and on my case. "You may not realize it 'cause I crack on you, but you're an okay guy. I just don't think these stories are good. You should stick with writing for the newspaper. Learn to accept your limitations."

I give Kirk a hard stare before exiting quickly so I can see Gabby play and feel better.

* * * *

My emotions push my foot hard on the accelerator as I head out on Owen Road. My hands are wrapped around the steering wheel as if it were Kirk's neck. I'm too angry to be scared or careful. As freezing rain pelts down, I'm not driving too fast or too slow, and things are not right as the Malibu skids off the expressway and smacks into the snow-packed shoulder.

I don't hit hard enough for the airbag to go off. Instead I manage to lodge my two front tires in the frozen snow hugging the shoulder of the expressway. Whatever faith in God I thought I'd lost, I regained as the car was heading off the road. I prayed harder in those eight seconds than I have in eighteen years. I try to get unstuck, but the car is in too deep. My life is metaphor rich. I sit for minutes that seem like hours, until I hear a tap on the windshield.

"You okay?" I hear someone shout in time with a louder tap.

I get myself together, trying to look like a man, not some stupid, reckless accident-prone kid, which is what I am regardless of what my driver's license says. A driver's license I won't need since I'm sure Dad will take it and end my driving days after this incident. I roll down the window. On the other side is a state trooper. I'm so scared I inhale half my lungs.

"License, insurance and registration please," she says.

It takes a second to get the documents, a second or two longer for my hands to stop shaking.

"You've been drinking?"

"No, Officer," I say, like I was competing for some obedience award.

"What happened?" she asks as she examines the documents. She's not really listening to the story, more interested in how I'm telling it. I hope my nervousness doesn't make me sound like I'm drunk or high. If being scared were a crime, she'd cuff me right now. When I finish, she doesn't ask me to get out of the car, but goes back to her cruiser.

The icy rain stops while I wait. I'm stuck spinning on the big wheel of 'what if'. What if I'd left the meeting ten minutes earlier, then would this slick spot have been on the road? What if Myrtle hadn't run outside just as Daisy was driving by in Gatsby's car?

"Put it in reverse," she says when she returns to the car. I do, but the front tire's lodged in the snow, while the back tires spin on the slick pavement.

"I'd better get some help or wait until the spring thaw," I crack. She doesn't react.

"You can't leave your car here. It's too dangerous. You'll need a tow truck."

She doesn't ask me why a smile appears on my face "Call All Star Towing in Fenton. I know the owner." As she makes the call, I wonder what the punishment is for lying to a state trooper.

* * * *

The officer stays with me until a red, white and blue tow truck arrives. A tall African American man gets out of the truck. He speaks with the officer, then comes toward my car. He wears a Detroit Lions wool cap, thick black gloves and an aura of authority.

The tow guy walks past my door, looks at the car then finally comes toward me.

"You have insurance?" he asks with a deep voice. I nod like a puppy dog.

"Does it cover towing? If not, fifty dollars cash." He seems in a hurry.

"I don't have any money." I sigh.

"Welcome to Fenton," he says, then smiles. Gabby's smile. "If you don't have any —"

"I go to high school with your daughter," I say, quickly, so I don't stumble.

"My daughter?" He looks confused, not confrontational.

"Gabrielle Gibson, right?"

"How do you know that?"

"I've seen you at her games. I write about girls' sports for the Fenton school paper."

"What's your name?"

"Carson Banks."

"You wrote those articles about her being all-state in three sports, right?"

"That was me, sir."

"I owe you," he says, smiling Gabby's smile again. "Every time after we submit an application for college, I mail the athletic director a copy of that story, so keep writing."

"I will keep writing," I say. "You know, I was going to her game when this happened."

"So was I," he says. "Except you're not the only accident, so I gotta keep working."

"If I get out of this and see her, I'll let her know I ran into you. Well, ran off the road."

"You're funny, kid," he says, then laughs. Gabby's laugh.

"Can I watch you hook it up?" I ask. As I walk with him toward his truck, I tell him about my dad repairing machines and always making me watch whenever he does it. I'm having a bonding moment with a man whose daughter I love, and he doesn't have a clue.

He gets the car unstuck and pointed back in the right direction. I need to get moving to not miss Gabby's game. I need to stay to not miss this opportunity.

"What are her plans after high school?" I ask, acting innocent. "Going right to the pros?"

"She wants to go to college in California, so we're working on scholarships," he says.

"She doesn't want to stay in Michigan?" I probe deeper. "Nothing to keep her here?"

"Like what?" he says, very sharp.

I look at the ground, hiding my smirk. "Like what if she had a boyfriend or something?"

"She doesn't have time for nonsense like that," he says. I look up and his friendly smile has turned into a clenched jaw. I don't think anyone's looked at me as hard as he's doing now.

He thanks me again for writing about Gabby as I climb back into my car, which I now wish was that Delorean from those old movies where 'what if' and the past could be changed.

Chapter Twenty-Eight

Friday, January 21st

"What's going on?" I whisper as Gabby slams the palm of her big black hand against my skinny tan locker. We're in the crowded hallway. At school during the daytime, we act like acquaintances, while in the back seat during the night, we get entangled in each other. We never ever talk like this in public.

"Carson, how could you?" Words squeeze from her mouth through a frozen jaw.

"What did I do?" I ask. I know I'm getting called for my charging into her home life foul by talking with her father.

"Don't speak to me." The words sharp, the laser beam narrowed eyes sharper still.

"The thing with your dad?" I laugh. She blows our cover and pokes me hard in the chest. A few people turn and stare. Do I hear the Fenton High rumor machine starting to whir?

Her non-answer is her answer. She's got on her game face. Gabby stares at me like I was an opposing forward. She's nothing but muscle, intimidation and scorn.

"Sorry I didn't write the whole article about you, Gabrielle," I say way too loud as she stomps away from me. Each smack of her Chucks against the floor feels like a slap in the face.

"Good thing she didn't slam dunk me into my locker," I say to those watching the scene. Nobody laughs. I don't blame them. I'm shaken up since Gabby's never been mad at me before—getting her angry makes me sad and scared. What if I'd, for once, just shut my mouth? What if.

"Carson, you okay?" Tim asks, arriving at our shared locker. I've got bags under my eyes from not sleeping, worrying about Caitlin. He's got a full book bag from prepping for the future. Hearing Caitlin talk about life has made me more anxious for a happy ending to her story.

I've kept most everything about Gabby to myself and away from Tim since he's still mateless. There's no need to rub romance salt in those lonely guy wounds, in particular around Valentine's Day. A day that never mattered before—a day I probably just ruined. "I'm all good."

"Let's find some time to hang out," Tim says, more than a little hurt in his voice.

I nod, promise him and myself. Like the other promise I made, to bring Caitlin home, turned out to be a lie, I'm sure this will be, too. Is a promise a lie if it doesn't come true, or is it something worse?

"Sure, Tim." Another promise I say that I'll slay. Although from the tone of Gabby's voice, I should have white space on my calendar for Tim since Gabby's burning red. No wonder in porn people go right to fucking after saying hello. It is easier than relationships in real life.

* * * *

"I messed up," I tell Charlotte in the last few minutes of journalism class, which has broken down into cliques—photographers, other staff and seniors like me, Kirk and Charlotte. Kirk's reading Josh's column aloud to anyone who will listens. If Gabby's steps were slaps, each laugh at Josh's sarcastic Valentine's Day essay—'YVD?'—is a kick below the belt. I've never been in a fight, but this morning gives me an idea of what it feels like to get beat up.

Charlotte and I huddle near Mr. Jakes' desk. He's out among the people, well, mostly the nerdy freshman girls hanging on Josh's every written word. I finish telling Charlotte about Gabby being mad at me. Charlotte's shaking her head like she had a swivel instead of a neck.

"So, I need you to broker peace," I whisper. "Just get Gabby to talk to me."

More head shakes. I should get a basket to catch Charlotte's head when it twists off.

"Charlotte, say something, or maybe you agree with her dad that this is all nonsense." Like school dances I can't attend, like jobs I can't get, like sisters I can't rescue, like all of my life.

Charlotte takes a quick look at the clock—two more minutes—and snatches the two hall passes from Mr. Jakes' desk. "Let's go outside," she says, and motions for me to follow her.

We slip out of the door — Mr. Jakes oblivious as usual — and stand in the hall. Inside the room I hear laughter, while I'm fighting to hold back tears. "Is she breaking up with me?"

"Look, Carson, I don't know anything," Charlotte says. Our backs are against the wall, hers literal, mine metaphorical. "Gabby and I… It's just not that kind of friendship. Since you two got together, she's never confided in me about you. So, I wish I could, but I can't help you."

"Yes, you can. At lunch, find her. Ask her to meet me in the library."

Charlotte pauses, keeping me waiting and frustrated, something she excelled in for years. Above us, a clock clicks off time way too loudly. "Okay, but you need to do something for me."

"Anything," I blurt.

"Stop hating on Josh."

The bell rings right on time. Josh is the bell telling me that I'll never make it. Josh is to me what Dwayne was to Caitlin, the destroyer of my distorted dreams. Caitlin's unreachable goals landed her on a stripper pole and in porn. Where will my unquenched thirst leave me?

"I'll do my best," I say, wondering if I even know what that word means anymore.

* * * *

"Carson, I'm so angry at you."

Charlotte got her to meet with me. It's a start.

I've apologized now into the double digits, but it's getting us nowhere. We're in one of the small study rooms. In the library, people study for tests. In here, I'm failing at life and love.

"When I got home, my dad asked all these questions about you." She makes eye contact with the table. She sniffs, but doesn't sob. She bends, but doesn't break. "And I had to tell him so many lies. I hate, hate, hate having to do that. I feel like I'm letting him down, again."

"Gabby, it's your life, not his," says the man who has let another person's life shadow his decisions for the past three years. "Why don't you tell him the truth?"

"No."

"But then we could go to the dance in February, be a normal couple." I reach my hand across the table. Gabby responds by folding her arms across her chest, tucking her hands in her armpits. "I mean, are you ashamed of me? Am I too weird? Too normal? Too whatever?"

"The world is not all about you, Carson Banks." Her hands stay tucked away yet she can still slap my face. "I have my reasons and I have—"

"No, Gabby, you have your secrets. I want you to share them with me."

Her arms uncoil like two brown snakes and her hands slam against the table so hard the glass of the room vibrates. "My body is all you want me to share with you."

I make the timeout sign, but she's revved up. "You think I'm a slut, right? 'Cos of the stuff we do. Guy does it, he's a stud, but a girl does it, she's a slut." Another timeout sign, the fingers on my left hand jabbing into the palm of my left. "It is *my* body. I decide, not you."

I flinch like she's thrown a punch because it reminds me of the message Caitlin sent to me when I saw her in LA. "Gabby, where is this coming from?" I ask.

"I guess after the thing with my dad, after you telling me that you told Tim about us, that maybe, maybe, Carson, I cannot trust you. If I can't trust you, I don't want you to touch me."

I wipe my hands against my sweating forehead then press down my uncombed hair. I'm not male model material, but this morning I look like an unkempt icon. When Gabby wouldn't pick up the phone last night, I knew something was wrong, so little things like sleep and hygiene got hijacked by worry. I suspected bad, but not this—the worst.

"What do you have to say?"

"Gabby, I love you, and I know that sounds so cliché, but it's true, so it's natural that I should, I mean, that *we* should…" I run out of words, not a good trait for a would-be writer. Oh, wait, I'm a failure at that, too. "Tell me what I need to do to earn your trust."

"You're suspended for four weeks, Carson," Gabby sighs. "Benched from my body."

"Suspended?"

"You can look, but you can't touch. We can talk, but not like before. If this is really about me—Gabby Gibson, the whole person—then you can prove it, but if it's just about you…"

I reach my hand out and dramatically offer her a handshake. "Last touch for four weeks."

For the first time today, she smiles. For the last time in four weeks, I feel the press of her skin against mine. "Well, I guess the only person happy about this will be my father."

"Your father?" Gabby asks.

I've yet to let go, our palms both sweating. "It will lower our energy costs, as I predict four weeks filled with cold showers."

Chapter Twenty-Nine

Saturday, February 12ᵗʰ
Valentine's Day dance

"You'll call if you need us, right?" Mom says, clipping on earrings. "I left the number."

"Mom, stop worrying. I can handle being in the house alone." Mom doesn't fully trust me, probably because Caitlin threw a party whenever my parents went anywhere overnight. Dad's lost faith in me as well, thanks to my accident. He's taken away my car keys for longer than Gabby took herself away.

They're headed to a party at a union hall in Flint, then spending the night at a motel. It's both Valentine's Day and their anniversary, which proves either great timing or greater frugalness. I'm at home because my sex suspension isn't over for a few more days. Gabby's acting distant, while I'm growing desperate.

For me, this night proves that the greatest writer — other than Fitzgerald — was wrong. Screw you,

Shakespeare, it is *not* better to have loved and lost than never to have loved at all. The three previous Valentine's Day dances, I didn't have anyone to go with, and it was sad, but not painful. It would be much worse to go blind than to be born without sight. You know what you're missing. I have to be with Gabby tonight. I call from the kitchen, home of serious talks.

"Hello," she answers. My heart almost blocks my throat from responding.

"Gabby, it's Carson. Please listen." I wait to hear the click. It doesn't come. "I know I'm still benched, but I want to see you tonight so bad."

"How can I trust you Carson?"

"Other than Tim, I've not told a soul. And I know you told Charlotte, so we're even," I remind her. "Besides, this isn't working out too well for you, is it? I watch the games."

Purity is screwing my life, which is bad, but it's messing with her game, which is worse. Are her dreams going to crash and burn like mine? Like Caitlin's?

"Why can't we go to the dance? Why can't people know about us?"

"You know why," she says.

"I know what you tell me," I say, then shoot the three. "This has nothing to do with black and white. I think you're lying to me. What's really going on?"

There's the clicking sound, followed by the dial tone. I don't even bother to call her back. I grab the spare set of car keys Mom hides in the kitchen, violate Dad's no driving rule and decide that I'll break my heart or Gabby's secrets tonight.

* * * *

Her dad's truck isn't in the driveway, but the lights are on in his room. I risk it all.

I pound on the door for ten minutes before she answers with just an angry stare.

"I see the lights on in your dad's room. Is he home?" I ask. Her non-answer tells me. "If you don't come out and see me right now, I'm coming in. And I'm telling him everything."

"That would be a mistake," she says.

"I've made a lot of those. I'm good at it," I snap. "Don't I deserve a second chance?"

"I knew you'd play that card." She makes a sound, something between a laugh and a cry. "I don't like going back on my word. I said four weeks, and—"

"I'm sorry, Gabby. I don't know what else to say to you other than I love you."

Her brown eyes narrow as she stares me down. "You say that but—"

"I don't want to just say it," I whisper. "I want to show you. Let me show you."

Gabby says nothing, but it's almost as if I can see the wheels turning in her head as she's trying to decide what to do. I offer my hands to her, but she doesn't take the bait. "Please, Gabby, let me show you."

She turns away, so I step across the threshold and gently place my hands on those strong shoulders that carry her team. I move closer, my mouth next to her right ear. "Give me a second chance."

I back away, put my right hand on her chin. A smile finally emerges, followed by the click of her locking the door. She follows me toward the car and there's another click, that of the Malibu's door opening. Then the clicking of my heart against my chest when she climbs in.

"Does a second chance mean a happy ending?" Gabby asks as she clicks the seatbelt. The clicking stops when our lips fit together perfectly once more.

I put the car in Drive and speed away. "Where are we going?" she asks.

"We're not going to the school dance. Don't worry."

"Good, I'm not dressed for it." She's wearing her usual hoodie, T-shirt and jeans.

"That's okay. Where we're going, you don't need to be dressed," I whisper.

"What do you mean?"

"I can't stop thinking about being with you." My heart and head accept the limitations on our love, but the monster wants what it wants. "Don't tell me you don't feel the same."

She doesn't say anything, which says everything.

"I want you as bad as I've wanted anything in my life."

She leans against me, kisses my cheek, then latches onto my arms like a drowning person clutching a rope. She's not drowning, but I sense she's holding back tears. I'm not sure if they're tears of anger, fear or happiness. Like all of our emotions, I suspect it's a mix tape.

The rest of the drive, there's little conversation. She calls her dad and lies to him about being with friends. Unlike me, it seems to pain her to lie. "I need to be home by midnight."

"I just need you," I whisper back. She leans against me all the way to my house.

"Where's the bathroom?" she asks as I lead her in the house, toward my bedroom. I point and she disappears inside. While my parents are not supposed to be home until the morning, I play it safe and unlock the window in case we need to abort. I turn off the lights.

"Carson, I'm not sure," Gabby says as she comes into the room. She's still dressed.

"Lock the door," I say, and she complies. I take off my shirt. I'm always a role model.

"I didn't plan on this," she says, then slips off her hoodie, then her white T-shirt.

"We'll just let it happen." I guide her into the bed. The room's dark with just a ray of white light from the moon illuminating our way. "We'll take it slow, like you want."

Just like times before, we kiss for a long time. Her tongue tickles the rough of my mouth. I still fumble with her bra, which always makes her laugh. That's not the sound I want tonight.

She rolls on top of me and starts kissing my chest, lowering herself. She starts to unsnap my jeans, but I reach down and stop her. "Carson, what's wrong?" She moves up the bed.

I respond with a flurry of soft kisses and gentle licks. I flip positions, and now I'm on top and moving down her body inch by inch. I undo her belt, but she resists. "Gabby, just relax."

"Carson, no," she whispers as my tongue traces small circles down her body.

"This might take a while at this pace," I whisper. "You know, because—"

"I'm tall for a girl," she whispers back.

"And I'm enjoying every inch." I unhook her belt, unsnap her jeans, and slide them down. She lets me pull her panties down, my fingers brushing against her curly pubic hair.

"Carson, wait—" she starts, but stops when I put my mouth on her. She moves her hips and my crappy old bed creaks, but that's the only sound for a long time until finally she moans.

"Let me make you happy once. Trust me." All my words are whispers now.

"Go slow," she says, so softly I can barely hear her, which is amazing given that all five of my senses are working overtime with taste and smell racing in front.

"That's nice," she whispers. Minutes later, a moan says, 'more'. Then the moaning stops.

"I'm sorry," I say, looking up toward her, "I don't really know what I'm doing."

"It doesn't seem like it. It feels nice."

"I've never done this before," I confess.

She breathes in deeply, then says, "Contrary to popular opinion at school, neither have I." I have to stop because I'm too busy laughing. It takes me a second to compose myself before I can start again. Instead, she pulls me up toward her. "That's enough, Carson."

"So, you're ready," I say as I open the drawer next to the bed where the condom is stashed.

"Carson, don't be angry," she says, her voice muffled.

"Did I say something? Do something? I didn't hurt you, did I?"

"No, this is perfect," she says as I nuzzle against her. "I just can't."

"What's wrong, Gabby?" I snap. For once, I'm doing things right, and she's still upset.

"Maybe I was wrong to even do this. When I first met you, I thought you were so gentle," she starts. We're eye to eye, but hers are watering. "I didn't think you'd act like this."

"Act like what?"

"Another one of those guys who get all angry at their girlfriends because they won't—"

"I'm not angry at you because you don't want to have sex," I say and sigh. "I'm angry because you won't tell me why. I'm angry because you won't let me into your life. Let me in."

She doesn't answer, so I let the darkness and silence and beating hearts fill the void.

"You always say that you want to trust me, and I've done my best." I flick my fingers gently over her exposed stomach. "But you need to do the same for me. You need to trust me. You need to tell me. You need-"

"The reason I got so mad at you about my dad and the reason I won't have sex with you, it's all related. It's all a bunch of lies. I'm sorry, I should have told you this, but—"

"But what?" I sit up, but she pulls me back down next to her. Skin to skin for a long overdue heart to heart.

"I didn't want you to think badly of me because of my past," she says, starting to cry.

"Your past?"

"When I lived in the north end of Flint, before we moved out here... I got pregnant. I was fourteen."

I can't decide what to ask first—why? Or who?—so I shut up.

"He was older, a friend of my cousin's," she says. "He made me feel special, but he was a player. When I told him I'd missed two periods, it was the last I heard from him or my cousin."

"So, you have—"

"No," she says, then goes silent.

"I couldn't tell my mom," Gabby says. "She would have called me a slut. I knew it."

"So you told your dad?" I ask.

"It was the hardest thing I've ever done."

"What did he say?"

"Nothing," she answers. "He just stared at me. He could've punched me in the face and it wouldn't have hurt—or left a mark as deep—as that look. I never want to see that look on his face again. His eyes were so hard, so angry, so filled with rage, betrayal, disappointment."

While my arms never leave Gabby, my brain races to images of the looks on my parents' faces if I told them that Caitlin Banks is now Callie Bangs. Lies hurt—truth destroys.

"We went out of town, like he was ashamed, but I wasn't ashamed. I was just afraid," she continues. "Afraid of going to the clinic, afraid of making the only choice I could and yet just as scared of what my life would be like if I didn't."

I'd have pulled her closer if the laws of physics would have allowed it.

"All my dreams, all his dreams, all of it, I knew, would be gone if..." she says. The word 'if' acts like lightning and knocks out the power to the conversation and all that is left is the beating of our hearts. Nothing is like I imagined it, but the distance between the dream and daily life doesn't devour me, it brings me comfort. I start to speak, but she silences me.

She's right, again. There are no words too hard or too soft. Everything is just right. I can't do anything about Gabby's sad past, so I know I need to give her—and Autumn—a happy ending.

Chapter Thirty

Excerpt from Autumn's Fall
'Valentine Visit'

"August, are they out?"

August was too stunned to speak upon hearing his sister Autumn's voice for the first time since she shouted 'I hate you' at their parents.

"They doing that silly anniversary ritual again?"

"Where are you?" August asked, the words tumbling out of his mouth in a panic.

"Across the street. Can I come in for a minute?" Autumn asked.

August thought, even if she was across the street, she sounded lost. And she had been, but now she was found. August raced toward the front window, threw open the drapes and saw Autumn standing by a beat-up pick-up truck, without a coat, shivering in the bright star-filled eve. "Of course." He ran faster to the door, opening it and waving her in, his smile as big as the half-moon. She didn't wave back.

"One condition. You can't let them know I was here."

August paused, pondering which was more important—seeing his sister or obeying his parents. As he watched Autumn cross the street, he knew he'd need to cross a line, too. "I won't tell them. I promise." With that, Autumn hung up the phone and started toward the house. August flung open the door so hard it sounded like a gunshot.

Before August could say a word, Autumn hugged him tighter than he could remember, although he thought I'll always remember this moment, when my sister returned home.

"We were so worried about—" August started.

"I'm just here to get a few things. I'm not moving back home. I don't want to be here and they don't want me here." Autumn broke the hug. Autumn broke her brother's heart, again.

"I don't understand." August stood at the door, but felt like he'd been knocked on the floor. "I'm sure you could work something out with Mom and Dad."

"Not after..." she started, but stammered. Not after Christmas morning, August thought.

"I want a few things and then we're leaving."

"Dwayne?"

Autumn hugged his brother. "I told you. I dropped him after what he did to your dog."

"Thank you, but I forgave you," August whispered.

"But Mom and Dad... They won't forgive me about Grandma's money. I don't blame them. But I needed the money to get my career started." Autumn released the hug.

"Career?" August asked his high-school dropout sister.

"Troy, the guy in the car, knows people in New York who can get me started in modeling, but there are upfront costs — headshots, agent fees, new clothes and jewelry. It costs a lot, but it will be worth it when you go to the store one day and see me on the cover of a magazine."

"So you're moving to New York?"

"If you want to be famous, that's the place to be."

"Why?" August asked the one-word question that had haunted him for years.

"Why do I want to be famous?" Autumn answered, sounding bemused by the query. She pointed at the big screen TV. "I want to be the one on TV, not looking at it. I want everybody in Fenton that treated me bad — which is just about everybody but you, August — to know they were wrong about me, especially Mom and Dad, always telling me to be realistic, be practical."

"But what if... What if it doesn't work out, modeling?" August hated sounding like his father, hated worrying like his mother, but mostly hated that he couldn't understand Autumn's life.

"Then I'll try something else. Then I—" Autumn stopped speaking when her cell phone buzzed. She glanced at it. "It's Troy. Our flight's in the morning. I took some of the money to buy us First Class tickets. I want to get used to living life like that."

"Is there anything I can say that would get you to stay?"

"Unless within the new few seconds you morph into a Hollywood producer, a TV director or a modeling agency owner, then no, August. There's nothing anyone can say." She smiled when she said it. It had been a long time since August had seen his sister's sober smile, even if the words she was saying crushed his hopes of him ever smiling again.

"So, like I said, I'm going to get a few things and then I'm gone."

"I'm sorry," August mumbled and started to sniff. "I'm sorry I ratted you out to Mom and Dad, but when you left on Thanksgiving, I was angry at you. I wanted to get back at you."

"I know I said stupid stuff about your immature shit, but that's because I'm so angry here all the time. I'm a rat in a cage in Fenton. I want to be a model on a runway in New York."

It wasn't a runway, just a flight of steps that Autumn climbed, each small step one step closer to her room than to her dreams, and one giant step farther away from August's life.

Chapter Thirty-One

Thursday, February 17th
Creative writing club meeting

"Is everyone ready?" Dr. Draper asks.

Almost everybody who started is back for today. She's announcing the winner of the best story and poem contest, which earns a small prize and will be the lead piece in the lit mag. The roses and razor blade girls are on pins and needles.

Gabby sits next to me. It's a home game tonight so she's here for me. She liked the story, but I couldn't bring myself, even in fiction, to be false. Happy endings are for kids, and both Gabby and I stopped being kids at fourteen when trauma first touched our lives.

"I'm pleased to announce the first prize story of this year's Fenton High School literary magazine is..." Kirk does a drum roll that gives me another reason to hate his guts.

"'She's Too Good for Me' by Josh Brown."

Charlotte gives Josh a huge hug. One of the razor blade girls wins the poetry prize. The others shred her with their black eyeliner glares. It's easier for me. I already resent Josh.

Josh describes the winning story about a smart, sensitive-type boy in love with a beautiful, mysterious girl. The BMG has a mental breakdown that tests the SSB's love for her. The SSB, of course, has a wacky sidekick — WSK — to tease and advise him. It's the same characters as in his other stories, except the names and quirks. Why tinker with success?

At Dr. Draper's urging, Josh reads from his prize-winning story, but I'm two thousand miles away from Fenton or fiction, thinking about Caitlin. When she's ready to come home, I'll still be in Fenton. I'm going to Baker in Flint, not Princeton. Josh and Charlotte will rule over Oberlin. Tim will be at MIT. Maybe I'm thinking about Caitlin because I feel this connection. Josh is Carol. I am Caitlin. I share the pain and rage of a total failure.

Josh's reading takes forever. The only good thing is how Gabby keeps staring softly at me. She won't let go of my eyes, although I don't understand why. She's a winner. I'm a loser.

When Josh finally finishes, the razor blade girl reads. As she does, one of her friends turns into an enemy and loudly leaves the room. I don't know why, but I follow her out.

"Hey, you, where you going?" I ask, desperately trying to remember her name.

"I quit." She jingles with the ten bracelets per arm parade when she talks.

"Why? Because you didn't win?" I ask. "Why can't you be happy for your friend?"

"Are you happy for Josh?" Bracelet Girl says with her tear-dripping raccoon eyes.

I don't owe her anything, I hardly know anything about her, she's a perfect stranger to me, so I tell her the truth. "He's not my friend. No, I'm not happy for him. I hate everything he is."

"I can tell." A small slit of white teeth shows between the thick black lipstick.

"It is so unfair." I sound like I'm eight, not eighteen. "He wins the contest. He's going to a good college, and he's born on third base." Maybe Kirk was right— *'Accept your limitations'*.

"I guess we're both losers."

"But I wanted this so bad," I say, almost crying at how deeply this hurts.

"Carson, you're a pretty good writer, but the things you write about are so unpleasant. I mean, maybe it's real, but it's too much. Why can't you write about something else?"

"I write how the world is," I say. "Josh writes how people want the world to be. I write about people who make mistakes. He writes about people with a quip always on the tip of their tongue contending for quote of the day. I'm about authenticity. He's Mr. Aspirations."

"Even so, the girl in your story is so messed up."

"You're sounding like Kirk," I interject. The insult doesn't faze her.

"No one deserves to have their own father hand them a gun to kill themselves," she says in teacher lecture mode.

"It happened. Everything in these stories is real. My dad really did that."

Her head jolts back as if I'd punched her jaw. "Seriously, Carson? I don't know what to say."

"Nothing. I just thought you should know."

"But I still don't understand something," she says in a hushed tone. "Why did you assume the dad gave the gun to the girl? It is implied, but the reader doesn't see it. Maybe Autumn wouldn't take the gun, so the father still has it."

"But he wouldn't pull the trigger like he was going to kill Autumn," I say.

"But he does pull the trigger, because August heard the click, right?"

I nod.

"And I guess we can assume that she doesn't know the gun isn't loaded."

Another nod.

"What if the reason Autumn runs away is because she watched her father put the gun in his own mouth and pull the trigger?" I glance up at the clock in the hallway. It ticks, so time is not standing still, it just feels that way.

So maybe it's Caitlin who can't forgive Dad, not the other way around. But what was it Gabby told me as I sat in the Excalibur parking lot and I understand even better now? That giving someone a second chance means forgiving them for their mistake, even if what they did hurt or disappointed you. It means you love them no matter what they did. If love is unconditional, then can it cure any condition—fear, shame and regret—like a magic drug?

Chapter Thirty-Two

Saturday, March 5th
Basketball semi-finals

"Daddy, you remember Carson?" Gabby says, trying to sound all calm.

Gabby, her dad and I sit in the stands at Fenton High, site of the state girls' basketball semi-finals. Fenton plays later this afternoon, but Gabby, her dad, the coach and a few other players showed up early to scout the possible competition for tomorrow if — I mean, when — they win later today. The finals are tomorrow at the sports arena.

"Sure, Carson," Mr. Gibson says as his big hand covers mine. It's loaded with the calluses of a working man. He doesn't squeeze hard, trying to crush me, so he must have believed every lie Gabby told him. "Hope your car made it. You covering the game?"

"As always, sir." I try not to crack even a smile or look at Gabby with lust in my eyes.

"Look over there, Gabs. You see those women?" Mr. Gibson says, pointing to the other side of the court. "Those are recruiters. I'm not sure from what college."

"I'm just gonna play my game," Gabby says.

Her dad smiles, but I hope he doesn't read behind the look on my face. He talks to his daughter about her future. I gaze at his daughter, remembering the recent past. How can I smell her scent and not remember her taste?

"If you do that," her dad says, "then they'll sign you up for sure."

"Here. These may help," I say, then open up my backpack and pull out a folder.

"What are these?" he asks. Gabby also looks surprised, which was my plan.

"No offense against the person who wrote girls' sports the last couple years for the paper, but they didn't do such a good job at making your daughter look as good as they could."

"I know that," he says, then smiles again at his daughter.

"I did some rewriting and reprinting." I hand him sports stories, which is my acceptance of my limits. "When she applies to colleges, you can include all of these stories I rewrote." Since I couldn't write a happy ending for Gabby, I created a happier past.

"We'll take these with us, won't we, Gabs?" he asks. She shrugs. Embarrassed.

"Take them where?" I ask.

"We're going to visit schools in California on Monday, first day of spring break," he says. "Gabs has always had California dreams, just like her old man, except she won't blow it."

I give Gabby my best sad 'don't leave me alone' look. It nicely covers the 'why didn't you tell me about this?' glare underneath. "My sister lives in San Diego. You going there?" I ask.

"There on Monday, then USC and UCLA on Tuesday, maybe some others," he says. "We'll end up at Long Beach State. They're a small school, but a sports powerhouse."

"I hope these articles help," I say, handing him the rest of the folder. It feels like I'm handing him a loaded gun. I've known it in the abstract, but it's never hit me until right now. Gabby's leaving. I'm staying. We're over. What did Carol say about learning to deal with loss? You get over it or it gets over you. It feels like I'm wearing an iron suit that weighs two tons.

* * * *

"Why didn't you tell me?" I say to Gabby when we sneak outside during half-time.

"I didn't know, not until this morning, really," she says. "He told me it was a surprise. It was our way of celebrating us winning the state championship."

"But you haven't won yet," I remind her.

"That's going to change by tomorrow. You watch."

"I wish I could be as confident as you."

"You can, Carson. Of course you can." I think she wants to sneak a kiss, but I see some NHS juniors, including Thien. I assume she's glaring at me big time through her tiny glasses.

"No, Gabby, I can't," I say. "I'm not arguing with you, just setting you straight."

"So, I'm good at sports, big deal. You're good at lots of things," she says.

"Name one," I demand.

She looks around like a spy making sure the coast is clear, then flicks her tongue against her top lip. "Okay, other than that," I say, blood rushing to and from my face at the same time.

"Okay, writing—you're good at that," she says.

"You mean for the paper," I say. "The stories are good because they're all about you."

"No, I meant your stories. Your novel about Autumn—"

"I'm done with that."

"What?"

"I'm done," I announce to myself as much as to her. Unrealistic ambitions hurl you in the wrong direction, like how Caitlin's star dreams led her to my computer screen. I've wasted so much time for so little results. The math doesn't work about words.

"What? Done writing? No, Carson, that's who you are. That's one of the things that—"

"When I heard Josh read his first story, I think I knew then I had to quit," I explain. "I knew then I wasn't the best, not even close. If I can't be the best, then why bother?"

"You can't quit something because you're not the best."

"That's easy for you to say, Gabby, because you *are* the best at something."

"For now, maybe. I know college ball will be harder. I don't plan on quitting then."

"So you don't mind being a loser?"

"My field goal percentage is fifty percent. I miss half the shots I take. I'm not perfect."

"I missed all my shots," I say. "I'm done wasting my time. I'll find some new dreams."

"Don't let guys like Kirk—"

"I don't have the talent or the temperament," I say, recalling Dr. Draper's words. "Maybe Kirk was right. If I can't be the best writer even at Fenton, how do I think I'd ever make it, especially up against guys like Josh who have everything going for them? I'm done."

"Carson, come on. Don't talk this way."

"Did you know in the morning before the alarm goes off that you actually hear a little click inside the clock? It's the click that wakes you up. Creative writing club was my click."

"Carson, but—"

"There'd be no pro athletes if there weren't people paying to watch them," I say. "Just the same, without readers, there would be no writers. I know my place now. I accept my limits."

"It was just one year, one club," Gabby says. "Give yourself a second chance."

Her father calls her name. As she walks away, I know that I have to follow her. Not now, but to California next week. I've given everyone a second chance except myself. I want a second chance with Caitlin now that I've learned so much in these past three months. She never called back or picked up, yet I know her birthday call was her way of keeping connected. But connections are not about wires, apps, vids, phones, texts, IMs or Facebook, but being face to face with someone as you each write the story of your lives. I need a second chance to give the book of Caitlin's life, my life, my parents' life, a happy ending.

While Gabby watches the game, I call Tim and ask him to meet me at the gym. As I wait, I call the Excalibur and learn Callie is dancing on Tuesday. I next call Southwest Airlines to get the info I need. I wait for Tim to get the money I need as well.

"Sorry I'm late," Tim says through heavy breathing. "When I was coming in, I noticed that NHS juniors are working the concessions and I noticed Thien was working, so..."

"*Méfiez-vous de la femme!*"

"What are you talking about?" he asks. "Did you go crazy since we last talked?"

"It's French for 'beware of woman'," I explain. "Thien speaks French. It was a joke."

"What's going on?" He's headed on Monday to check out MIT.

"When you go away, are you taking a computer?" I ask.

"What are you talking about?" He seems confused. I don't blame him.

"Would you like to buy my Mac? I know you want it. I'm done with the online world."

"I already have a computer for college," he says, but I have my best begging eyes staring right at him until he finally asks, "Okay, how much?"

"Six hundred." I don't tell him that's the price of the plane ticket, a hotel and money for food.

"For a four-year-old Mac?"

"Please, Tim. I need your help."

"You could just ask me for the money, Carson," he says. "I'd loan it to you."

"I can't ask you for money. My dad says never let money come between best friends."

"Carson, no offense, but we really haven't been best friends for a while," he reminds me as he stares at the floor. "You got involved with the paper, creative writing and Gabby."

"I'm sorry, Tim, but about the Mac... Whatever you're willing to pay."

"Like I said, let me just loan you the money."

"I need to earn the money! I want you to buy something from me and this is all I have!" Images of Callie Bangs dancing on stage and fucking on my screen click in my head.

"Okay, I'll buy it, but only if you do something for me," Tim says.

"Anything."

"I decided to ask Thien to prom, but I know she won't go with me, if..." He lets it dangle like a piñata. I need to hand him the club.

"If she thinks we're still friends," I finish it. "Why don't you just tell her that we're not?"

"I don't want to lie to her," he says. "I mean, is that any way to start with someone?"

I've soaked myself in so many lies, I can't answer that. "So what can I do?" I ask.

"I don't know, but I do like her and I think she likes me," he says, then we both go silent.

I realize my dark past with Thien can help with Tim's bright future. "Let's go see her."

"Don't embarrass me in front of her," Tim says, but I'm in a full fast walk mode. We stand a few feet from where Thien works with a few other NHS girls. Tim waves. She waves at him. She sneers at me, and it's time that Tim knows why. I step next to him, start it and end it.

"If you go to the prom with her, from experience, don't plan on getting laid or even blown."

"Carson, don't talk like that." Tim takes a step back.

"She's going to tell you about last year's prom, if she hasn't yet," I say, now in a whisper.

"I don't care what happened last year," Tim says.

I offer up my hand for him to shake and seal the deal for him to buy the Mac.

I pause for a second. I think about Tim, the meaning of friendship, the money I need, and I decide this is a case where the means to the end isn't another lie, but for once, the truth.

"You promised me the money. You won't back out?" I ask as he returns the handshake.

"I won't back out," Tim says. "What can I say so she'll believe we're not friends?"

"She wouldn't even give me a hand job, so—"

"Carson, that's enough, stop it!" he shouts. Thien and her friends are staring at us now.

"So I say fine, and we start making out again. Then when it's time, I pull down my pants, and like I'd seen in porn, I gave her goo glasses by jerking off in her face."

Tim pushes me and I hit the floor. Caitlin would have been proud of my acting. Just as Thien—who is running toward Tim, not me—must be proud of Tim. As I pick myself up, I suppress the crooked smile that comes with an order of ends and means.

* * * *

"I can't believe it," Gabby repeats every ten seconds as we burn up the phone deep into Sunday morning. She doesn't need to worry about getting a good night's sleep because the Lady Tigers won't be playing in the state championship game Sunday afternoon.

"You played great, but you couldn't do it alone," I say, and it's not just flattery. When Fenton's playmaker guard went down with an injury, there was no one to get the ball to Gabby. With Cass Tech double-teaming her, Great Gabby or not, Fenton's fate was sealed.

"But I lost," she says. I'm sure not wanting to cry in front of me is one of the reasons we're not together tonight. But she said she needed to be with her team, then later with her dad. It gave me time to come up with a cover story about visiting Tim in Boston over break.

"There's no 'I' in the word lose, but there are two 'I's in the sentence, 'I still love you, Great Gabby'. You're the greatest Great Gabby ever."

"Carson, doesn't your back hurt from shoveling so much bullshit?" she cracks.

"Maybe so. Maybe you can come over here and rub it for me?" I say. "Then maybe there's something of yours I can—"

"Carson, I just lost my last high-school basketball game and you want to talk about—"

"Fine, I'll change the subject," I cut her off. "I'm flying into Los Angeles next week."

"Look, you can't come with me and Dad to visit—"

If I can lie naked next to Gabby, it's time to come clean. "Caitlin lives in Los Angeles."

"What! How long have you known that?"

"Over Christmas I went to see her, tried to get her to come home, but I failed," I say. "So, like you said how everybody deserves a second chance, I'm giving myself a second chance to say the right things to get her home, or I guess believe that she's really happy out there."

Gabby goes silent and I enjoy sharing it with her. "Where does she live in LA?"

"I don't know. I just know where she works."

"Where?"

"Are you sitting down?" I ask.

"Why?"

"Because I have a story tell you," I start. It takes me about half an hour to tell Gabby everything about Caitlin I've learned since homecoming. I confess even to how I found the photo.

When I get to that part, she interrupts me, "Carson, that's gross."

"Gabby, there's a name for a teenage boy who says he doesn't jerk off to Internet porn."

"What's that?"

"A liar."

She laughs. "Well, I'll be in need of a good lie to tell my dad when it's time to go to UCLA about why I need for him not to be there with me."

"Why do you need that?" I ask. "Where are you going to be?"

"With you," Gabby says. "I'm going to help you bring Caitlin home and get the happy ending that everybody wants."

Chapter Thirty-Three

Tuesday, March 8th
Second day of spring break

"Do you have any money?" Gabby asks me almost the minute she gets out of the cab.

"I'm tapped," I tell her. "I'm not sure how I'll get back to the airport."

"Maybe I'll take a bus back," she says.

"When is your dad expecting you?" My folks think I took the bus to Boston to see Tim.

"He thinks I'll be back at the hotel by nine p.m." I look at my watch. It's three-forty-five p.m. I've been here all afternoon, mostly sitting on the grass near the parking lot. Other than a few drunks asking for change, or a guy looking to sell me weed, everybody's left me alone.

"Gabby, I'm sorry I got you into this."

"I want to be here," she says, grabbing my hand. It's almost shaking. She looks ashamed and more than a little afraid as men go in and out of the Excalibur show club. Never in a million years or two million alternate realities would I have ever imagined this scene—skinny white boy Carson Banks standing with his tall black girlfriend in the parking lot of a titty bar, waiting to meet his tattooed, pierced, stripper-nude model-porno actress sister.

Every car that turns into the parking lot, I will to be Caitlin's red Eclipse. I need the magic power to change colors, makes and models. I know it does no good, but sometimes I even pray. Pray for my sister to arrive at a strip club. That's how fucked up my life has become.

Gabby answers questions about colleges in her future while I wait to confront my past.

"That's her car," I whisper to Gabby, then point when the red Eclipse parks. Caitlin gets out of the car. Before the door even clicks shut, I'm running toward it, but stumble on the way.

"Caitlin," I call out, but she doesn't hear me. I see the buds in her ears, so I yell louder still. She's only a few feet from the back door, but she might as well be miles away. I pick myself up and run. Gabby, however, rushes past me. I wonder what Caitlin's eyes look like beneath those sunglasses when she sees this stranger grabbing her arm. I hope she's not carrying. There's a second of commotion, then Gabby turns to point at me. I'm out of breath by the time I reach them. Caitlin's sunglasses are off. Her hand is on her hip and she looks pissed.

"Carson, what are you doing here?" she spits out. "And who is this chick?"

"This is my girlfriend, Gabby," I say. Caitlin just looks confused as she stares at Gabby.

"Wow, does Dad know about this?" she asks.

"No," I answer. A look of sadness and shock consumes Gabby's face.

"Carson, what do you want?" Caitlin asks.

"I want a second chance," I say.

"At what?" Caitlin asks, almost spitting out both words.

"To convince you to come home with me," I plead. "You don't have to live like this."

"You don't know how I live." She says this like it should cut off the discussion.

"Prove to me you're really happy here and I'll leave you alone. We could go inside or..."

"You got a stack of bills?" she asks me, then turns to Gabby. "How about you?"

Gabby shrugs her powerful shoulders.

"No, I didn't think so," Caitlin says. "Well, if you don't have money, then nobody wants you inside. You'd just be taking up space for paying customers," Caitlin says.

"Fine," I say. "I flew all this way. Why can't you listen to what I have to say?"

"Fine," she replies. She turns her back on us and makes a call. A couple of 'fuck you, Larry's' later, and she says, "Let's go, Carson. I got things to do."

Caitlin turns on her high heels and starts toward the car. Gabby and I follow. Caitlin unlocks the car, and I hold the door for Gabby. "Where is she going?" Caitlin asks me.

"She's coming with us," I say. I drop my hand to my side. Gabby holds it tight.

"Why?" Caitlin asks.

I look at Gabby, then back at Caitlin. "Because I said so."

"Wow, big brother, you grew a sac," she says, then laughs. "Get in."

There's no conversation in the car. The rap music's up all the way up while the windows are all the way down. After we get off another of these endless expressways, my images of junkie-lined streets vanish under the palm trees. We pass through nice neighborhoods, then some scary ones. Near the end of the trip, the sun is blinding us coming in. We're headed due west, straight for the ocean. We pass by ugly apartments overlooking a strip mall parking lot. It reminds me a lot of where Carol lives. Then, we pull in on a beach road where Carol's sister, the stripper, drives into the parking lot of a tall, window-filled building near the ocean.

We're still not talking as we take the elevator up to the third floor, then head inside. The apartment is nicer than Carol's place, but messy just like Caitlin's room was back in Fenton. Every table overflows with celebrity magazines, every wall contains at least one mirror.

"This is nice," I say as I sit down. Most of the furniture is white, not Caitlin's usual red.

"It's okay," Caitlin says. "Once we get some real money, we're splitting up."

"We?" I ask. My 'we', Gabby, sits next to me on a big white sofa.

"One day, I'll be able to afford a place like this on my own, but for now I share it with two other girls," Caitlin continues. "They're away on a shoot this week."

I don't need to ask what kind of shoot. I wonder if the two friends are the same two girls I've seen in pictures with Caitlin—I mean Callie. Or are they the same person? I still don't know.

"You want some wine?" she asks as she walks into the kitchen. "Do you drink or what?"

"No, thanks," I say.

"How about you?" Caitlin says. "What's your name again?"

"Gabrielle," Gabby almost whispers.

"The Great Gabby!" I say in my sports announcer voice. Gabby looks embarrassed.

"What does that mean?" Caitlin opens a bottle of white wine. As she pours herself a tall glass, I testify to Gabby's exploits. Caitlin doesn't seem impressed or even interested.

"That's all well and good, but I got one thing to ask you," Caitlin says.

"What's that?" Gabby asks.

Caitlin walks back in the room, sits. "You treating Carson right?" she asks. Gabby smiles.

"She's being very nice to me." Our fingers are intertwined.

"Good, he deserves it," Caitlin says, then sips her wine. "He's a good kid. Not like me."

"Don't say that, Caitlin," I say. I know her secrets, but she doesn't know mine

"Why not? It's true," Caitlin says. "The problem with our family was all the lies. Mom lying to herself about some new career. Dad lying to himself that he was happy with his failed life. Carol's whole fucking goody two shoes perfect life was a lie. She was everything but nice."

"No, that's only part of it," Gabby says firmly. Caitlin shoots her a dirty look.

"Gabby, it's okay," I tell her.

"No, let the girl talk," Caitlin says. "You think you know something about me, about my life? You don't know shit about me."

"You're right, Caitlin, I don't," Gabby says, leaning in, looming larger. "I know about my life. I know about mistakes I made and how they almost cost me everything I wanted in life. But I got a second chance, and now I'm happier than I ever dreamed, thanks to your brother."

"I burned up all my second chances with my parents. I'm out of second chances."

"How about yourself?" Gabby asks. "Have you given yourself a second chance?"

"What are you talking about?" Another gulp.

"I got pregnant at fourteen," Gabby starts, then tells Caitlin her story, ending it with, "But I gave myself a second chance and now I make better choices. You could do that, Caitlin."

Caitlin gulps the rest of the wine. She's drinking at Dad's old pace. She sits the glass on a table, walks over to a desk and pulls out a big brown envelope, but still says nothing.

"Carson, I have a graduation present for you," Caitlin says finally, breaking her silence.

"What?" I ask as she stands in front of me, almost casting a shadow.

"This is for you." She pulls a pile of cash from the envelope and hands it to me. "One-k."

"Caitlin, I can't take this," I say, staring down at the wad of bills.

"Why? Because of how I earned it?" she says, looking hurt, not angry.

"No, that's not it," I say, not sure if I'm lying or not.

"Look, you flew out here to see me and I treated you like shit," she says. "And now you did it again. That must have set you back some bills. Let me do this for you."

"Take it, Carson," Gabby whispers in my ear. "She wants—no, she *needs* you to *do it*."

"Okay, thanks," I say, then stuff the cash in my pockets.

Caitlin then seals the brown envelope and hands it to me. "Give this to Mom and Dad."

I take it from her, it feels heavy. "How much is in here?"

"Five-k," she says.

"What for?"

"To pay them back for using Grandma's credit cards."

"Should I tell them it came from you?" I ask.

"No, you will never ever tell them about any of this, understood?"

"How do I explain suddenly having five thousand dollars?"

"Carson's a great writer. He'll think of something," Gabby says. I don't correct her.

"Are you going to college to write?" She points at me with her empty glass.

"I don't know anymore."

"Let's say you become an engineer like Dad wants, okay?"

"Okay."

She's headed back toward the kitchen. "So how is that different than what I'm doing?"

"Are you serious?"

"You're just using what you've got—your brain—to make it. You'll still be working for people you don't like, not making as much money as you want. How is that different than me?"

"Because I'd have my clothes on," I say. "Something everyone would be grateful for."

I see Gabby try not to laugh

"Funny, Carson, but my point is everybody's got different things they're good at, different things they want out of life," Caitlin says. "I wanted money and to be famous. I got some money, and one day I'll be a huge star. One day some Hollywood big shot is going come in the club, see me dancing on stage, put me on TV, and I'll be famous, just like I told everyone." Caitlin still dreams big, which makes me happy, but also a little bit sad.

Caitlin returns to her chair, glass refilled. "Gabby, what are your dreams for your life?"

"I don't know, maybe play professional basketball," Gabby says.

"You're going to use your body to make it. Why is how she uses her body, right?" she asks. We don't answer. "And why is how I use my body so wrong? Just answer me that."

I ponder as I look at Gabby, at the floor, then finally at Caitlin. Caitlin's got a point, but it's not the same and I bet she knows it. She's taking something that should be private and beautiful, like it is with Gabby and me, and making it public and ugly. I don't want Caitlin in this life but there's nothing I can do or say to change her mind about her body.

"Well, Carson?" Caitlin asks. I turn away, unable to face her until I can answer.

I stare at the white carpet as dark thoughts overwhelm me. My brain bounces like a tennis ball back and forth between feeling thankful but just as much regretful that I clicked on that image of Callie — not Caitlin, but Callie — back in October. I start to speak, but neither words wisdom materialize.

"How is it different?" Caitlin's transformed from stripper to inquisitor.

I lift my head, sigh, force a sad smile, then say softly, "It just is, Caitlin. It just is."

"You should go!" she snaps. "I don't judge your dreams or your life. Don't judge me."

"Caitlin, I'm not judging you. I'm judging me," I say softly. "Can we get a ride?"

"Call a cab. You've got a thousand dollars. Unless it drives you home, you'll get where you're going."

"Before I go, can I ask you one thing?" I ask as we get up to leave.

"Fine, but that's it. After this, I'm a ghost. You wanna talk with me, you hire a psychic or a ghost whisperer. But don't call me and don't expect to hear from me. Understand?"

I nod, then stare her down as I ask, "On Christmas morning, what happened?"

"I don't want to talk about that, it is private!"

"You dance in front of strangers naked but you tell me this is private?" I ask. "I was there at the top of the stairs. I heard it, but I need to know the details. I need that chapter of the story to be closed. Maybe if I understood why you left I could have —"

"Enough, Carson, enough," Caitlin says, the first 'enough' hard like's she's angry, the second one soft as if exhausted.

For the first time, Caitlin looks ready to cry. For some reason, from the sniffing sounds coming from Gabby, she's beaten Caitlin to it. I continue, "So, I heard what Dad said. I heard you say '*I hate you*'. I heard a pistol click, and then you were gone. Who was the gun aimed at? Who pulled the trigger?"

Caitlin stares at the floor, but it doesn't open and swallow her when she says, "I did."

"Who were you pointing the gun at?" Mom's and Dad's faces flash before my eyes.

Caitlin bites her bright red bottom lip. "I thought the gun was loaded. I was so angry at them. I wanted to punish them. I put the gun against my head and pulled the trigger."

Gabby cries hard and wet, like a soaking spring shower. I hold her hand tight. It helps keep my own hand from shaking.

"I'd fucked up so bad, stealing from Grandma. While they might have forgiven me, they'd never forget that. Nor would I." She pauses, takes a drink, and continues, "I'd dug a hole so deep I couldn't think of another way out. I put the gun to my head and I pulled the trigger. I thought it was loaded. I wanted to die. I was talking about myself when I shouted '*I hate you*'."

"But you didn't die," I say. "You're still alive, which means you could—"

"But I did, Carson. That's what you don't understand. That's what you need to understand," Caitlin says. "Your sister died that morning. I'm not Caitlin Banks anymore."

"You gave yourself a second chance by becoming a different person," Gabby says softly.

"I fuck for money, but that doesn't mean I'm fucking up my life," Caitlin says in a tone that tells us that's the last word. She sets down the again empty wine glass and walks us to the door. There are no hugs, tears or smiles. Caitlin shuts, not slams, the door behind us, making my life metaphor rich.

Gabby and I stay silent as we walk almost woundedly down the hall and as the elevator descends.

We're still silent as we start toward the exit. "What do you think?" Gabby finally asks.

"About what?" I start us walking—not toward the road, but out to the beach.

"About your sister?" She clutches my hand.

As we step out into the bright sunlight, I'm not just thinking about my sister. I'm also thinking about the past half-year and the ride home. Looking at Gabby, I think how in just six months one of my dreams has come true, while so many others have not. "So?" Gabby asks.

"This all started at homecoming," I say, then repeat the word. "Homecoming."

"She's not coming home. You know that," she says.

"I can still dream she'll come home. There's no harm in that," I admit, then fall into a void of silence and thought. If I follow Dad's goal for me and become an engineer, I know my first project. I will design a machine that separates the things you want into big black and white boxes labeled goals, promises, prayers, plans, dreams, delusions, ambitions and illusions. My machine won't run on electricity, but on the fuel of life—experience, loss and maybe redemption.

"I'm sorry, but it doesn't look like I'll be able to keep all my promises," I tell Gabby.

"What promises?" she asks.

"Well, the promise of the words 'I love you' I intend on keeping as long as I can, as much as I can, however I can," I say. "No, I'm talking about the other promise that I made to you."

"Other promise?" she asks.

"That Autumn's story would have a happy ending," I say as we reach the beach.

"Maybe you can't have a happy ending without a fresh start." Gabby points at the ocean. For all the ugliness of the last minutes, it's too beautiful not to notice. We share the silence.

There are no words left, just Gabby's dream moment and one memory—not the sound of Caitlin's words when she left home or the sight of Gabby's face when we are together. Not the sour envy smell of Josh Brown's genius or the sweet taste of Gabby's lips. No, the memory that lingers on my tongue this California twilight comes from a gray fall day. It's Dad and me working in a garage in Fenton, Michigan. He's teaching me about snowblowers. He's teaching me about life. He said, *"The work is good, and the parts fit together perfectly. Too loose, no click. Too tight, no click, just lots of grinding. But that clicking sound means it is just right."*

Soon, we'll move toward the street to find a taxi to start our journeys home. I can't help but think about the journey that Caitlin-Callie-Autumn is still on. Maybe it's not to find her way home, but just to find her way. One day—like a finger pressing a camera, like thumbs texting on a cell, like high heels on a hard floor, or like an empty chamber of a pistol—everything's going to click into place for Caitlin and be just right.

Chapter Thirty-Four

Sunday, April 5th

"I got into Long Beach State," Gabby says. "A full ride to an NCAA school."

"That's great." I'm trying to hide my frown, just like she's trying to hide her smile.

We're in her car, out by Lake Fenton. She kisses me as softly as she did that first time, at Charlotte's party. "Carson, we can make it work," she whispers.

"I believe you," I say. It doesn't matter whether it's a lie or truth because love is an act of faith.

"You should think about moving," Gabby says in a voice so small for someone so tall.

"Maybe." I pull her closer. Maybe is a great word because it's never a lie.

"You don't need to stay in Michigan."

"I know." I applied to a few colleges in Michigan, but nothing I'm excited about, although maybe because of the turnaround at GM, Dad might be going back to work.

"Both of your sisters live in California and—" Gabby starts, then her tongue clicks to a stop. Caitlin kept to her word. She's never called. She's not coming home. I've not kept the promises I made to myself but I'm breaking one to Caitlin. I'm going to tell my folks she's alive, to give them the money, to let them find peace. I told myself I was waiting for Caitlin, but that's the last lie I'll tell. I'm waiting for me, to find the same courage I showed locating Caitlin in order to tell my parents at least part of the truth.

"I'll think about it," I say, then go silent watching the sunset. It all seems too perfect.

"Have you thought of happy ending for your story yet?" Gabby asks.

"Not yet, but, I'm going to finish the story." Although I vowed I was done with creative writing club, I couldn't quit writing. Gabby, like that old song says, is my soul and inspiration. Part of shooting the ball, she always said, is knowing you might miss. But isn't it better to shoot, to try and maybe score, than to not even get out on the court? I'm writing, not for an audience, but for myself. Writing is a way of knowing, and I guess I still have a lot to learn. I'm not ready, like the character in Fitzgerald's *This Side of Paradise*, to announce, "I know myself, but that is all." I'll never be Josh Brown, but that's his loss because it means he'll never get a chance to be me.

"I told you I wanted a happy ending," Gabby says.

"Good thing writers can do that in fiction, since I didn't get one in real life." I don't tell her I've written her that happy ending—or as happy as I can view the world through a Caitlin-tinted lens. It will be my going away gift for Gabby.

"Carson, I wouldn't say that," she says. Her eyes move off the sunset and onto me.

"What do you mean?"

"You couldn't bring Caitlin home, but you tried," she whispers.

"I don't think there were any right things I could have said to her," I say, then sigh. "You know, in some way, all of this was never about her. It was about me."

"You?"

"To prove to myself I could try to fix our family. I failed, but I tried."

"What did I tell you at that party when we kissed the first time?" she says, then answers, "You miss one hundred percent of the shots you don't take."

"Well, actually the Great One said that. You just quoted him," I tease.

"But you said I *am* the Great One!" she says, acting all mock hurt.

"The Great Gabby!" We laugh, kiss, cuddle. It won't last forever, even if I move to Cali, but it is enough for now. Like the clicking sound of a seatbelt telling me I'm safe, the touch of Gabby's skin tells me everything is all right. Not forever, not in the past, but for now.

On the ride back into town, Gabby circles the McDonald's parking lot where Mom's Malibu awaits my return. She circles like she doesn't want this car ride to end.

"Gabby, is everything okay?" I ask.

"Carson, I'm ready," she says.

"Well, if you're ready, then we need to find a hotel," I crack. "Or my house."

"No, not for that," she says, then laughs. "I want us to go to prom, go public."

"Really?" I ask.

"Really," she says as that wonderful, if mischievous, grin spreads over her beautiful face. "But you know what that means, right?"

My face is all frown, no smile. "We have to sit with Charlotte and —"

I cover her mouth then clutch my throat like I'm choking. I cough loudly, roll my eyes, and hiss the name, "Josh."

"Everybody, even Josh, deserves a second chance," says the always-optimistic Gabby.

"Do you want to come meet my parents?" I ask.

"Not tonight, but soon, real soon," she says.

"Why the change of heart?"

"I guess I'm ready for my dad's disappointment."

"With me?"

"No, with me," she says. "He's got to know. He's got to accept me and my choices. Just like you need to tell your parents about Caitlin."

"Do you think he'll be mad?" I ask, avoiding her statement about Caitlin.

"Furious," she says. "More for lying than anything else, but he'll get over it. You can forgive most anything. You say you learned from me, but, Carson, I learned from you too."

"Well, there's a lot I want to teach you and —" I whisper.

"Carson, you're impossible," she says,

"No, *we're* impossible," I say, and she looks hurt. "Did you think you'd end up with someone like me? I never thought I'd love someone like you. Never thought I'd be so lucky."

She doesn't speak as she pulls the car into the parking lot. I kiss her, then start to open the door. "Please don't leave," she says. It's not the three words I want, but it's enough for now.

"That's what I should say to you," I say. "But you've got to pursue your dreams. Maybe I'll come to California, maybe I won't. You know your future, but I'm still figuring out mine."

"I'm sorry," Gabby says, or something like it. It's hard to tell because she's crying.

"Don't cry. Don't be sorry," I say. "We'll figure something out. I've taken two trips to California and come up empty-handed. Maybe the cliché is right. The third time is the charm."

"A lucky charm," she says, then kisses me soft, softer, softest.

I close the door as others open before me. As I get into my car and start home, I think how Gabby never says she loves me. She's the writer, not me. She doesn't tell. She shows.

* * * *

"I'm going to prom," I tell my parents as I sit down at the dinner table.

"That's wonderful, honey," Mom says.

"Carson, I'm going to start back to work soon, but we have a lot of bills," Dad says.

"I have the money. Don't worry about it," I say.

"Where did you get the money?" Mom asks. I'm a little hurt they're not asking who I'm going with, but we've been without money longer than I've been without a girlfriend.

I pause. I could say from Tim, but that would lead to more questions, which might lead to more questions, including the biggest one I have. He gave me the money, so why didn't he claim the computer? He's taking Thien to the prom. I wonder if I sold out my friendship or saved it.

"Carson, your mother asked you a question," Dad says.

I take a deep breath before I dive into the deep end. "From Caitlin," I say, as calmly as possible, which is impossible.

"Caitlin!" they both seem to shout at the same time.

"Caitlin's alive." I pause for them to catch their breath.

"Carson, you've talked with her?" Mom says.

"She's living in California."

"You've seen her?" Mom says.

"No, we've just talked on the phone," I lie.

"Why didn't you tell us?" Dad says, not angry, not sad, not anything but relieved.

"I promised her I wouldn't, but don't worry. She seems happy," I confess. I wanted her life broken so I could save her. I wanted her addicted to something other than star-struck dreams.

"I need to talk with her," Dad says. "To tell her how sorry I am about—"

"I promised her I wouldn't tell you how to contact her," I say.

"Carson, listen, son. You need to tell us so we can get her to come home," Dad says.

I pause. My parents' faces have gone from happy to hurt to hopeful, now back to hurt. This is the scene I've avoided since homecoming game night.

"Please," Mom says. "We could talk to her. We could—"

"I told her everything I could think of, but she's happy where she is."

"But—" Mom starts, but Dad reaches over to touch her hand. She squeezes his hand tight, like someone hanging on to a thread for dear life. And that's what I've given them, a thread of hope among my tangle of lies. They'd given up on this moment, so they can't respond to it.

"This is for you." I take the envelope from my pants and hand it to Mom. Tempted as I was, I left all the money intact. I took the thousand Caitlin gave me. I'll give Tim his money back, and I'll spend the rest on Gabby—on the prom this spring, on a flight to LA in the fall, or maybe moving there. I'm not sure of my next step, but this conversation is an overdue start.

Mom looks surprised when she opens it, her tear-filled eyes wide and wet.

"It's to pay back the money she ran up on Grandma's credit card," I say. "She wanted me to tell you how sorry she was. I told her that you'd forgive her, not because she paid it back, but because she said she was truthfully sorry. If I talk to her again, can I tell her that? Can I?"

I look at Dad's wet eyes. Behind the eyes, I imagine, he sees the movie of Caitlin's life—her birth, childhood, teen trauma and disappearance. Does he hear the click of the gun?

"Can you forgive her?" I ask again.

My parents look at each other, but say nothing. Twenty plus years of marriage allows them to communicate without a sound. Finally, Dad—it has to be Dad—says, "We all made terrible mistakes. If she can forgive us, then we can forgive her."

"Forgive you?"

"Carson, you can't know what we've felt, losing a child like that," Mom adds. "It would be one thing if she'd died, but she disappeared. There's no worse feeling for a parent than not knowing. You can only imagine fates worse than death." If I ever doubted my decision not to tell my parents about Caitlin's new life, these words washed them all away. I protected them.

"If I talk to her again, I'll tell her," I say in what I hope is my last lie. I know I'll never see Callie Bangs or anyone like her on my computer again. That's behind me, I pray. I doubt I'll see Caitlin Banks either. Maybe we'll talk on the phone, maybe we'll never talk again. She's not Caitlin anymore, but she was once. Now she's someone else. She's just a stranger I used to know.

"Maybe she'll come home one day," Mom says loudly. Dad and I nod in agreement.

I'm pretty sure there'll be no homecoming, just like I doubt I'll ever become the bestselling author I aspire to be—or even as great as Josh Brown, but I'll hang on to these dreams, hopes, aspirations or whatever they need to be called for a while longer. If we don't have dreams in our lives, that just leaves us with nightmares. Sometimes the nightmares are what we don't know, sometimes they're what we know and fear. Maybe the only thing to fear isn't fear itself, but letting your dreams die or allowing your dreams to destroy you. In these trips between Michigan and California, in these encounters between my past and my present, in these possible futures presenting themselves to me, I've covered plenty of miles. I'm not tired. Instead, I'm stronger because I've narrowed the distance just a little between who I am and who I want to be.

Chapter Thirty-Five

Autumn's Fall
'Easter Arrival'

August felt the phone vibrate in his pocket as he walked in the parking lot with his parents after exiting St. John's Church, a place where none of his prayers had ever been answered.

He didn't recognize the phone number — seven-one-six area code.

His father, who refused to get a cell phone, rolled his eyes. His mom said nothing. They weren't taking to each other. August wondered why they bothered to talk with him, but maybe their silence was God's punishment for not telling them about Autumn's Valentine's Day visit.

The voice on the phone said, "August, it's Autumn. Can we talk?"

August froze like ice in the spring sun. "I need to take this," he told his parents.

"And I need to get home before the first pitch." His father pulled out his keys and shook them loudly like some dungeon master. "Your geeky friends shouldn't be calling on Easter."

Since Autumn left, August seemed to have no friends anymore. "I'll walk home."

August's dad laughed, while his mom shook her worried face then said, "It's too far."

Gritting his teeth, August repeated his intention. "Get in the car," his father said.

August paused, his world as upside down as his phone. He couldn't say no to his father, so instead he turned his back and started walking away from the car. His father yelled at him to return, but August kept walking. His mom yelled as well, with no results. August thought, How do they know I won't just keep walking, like Autumn? "One second," he said into the phone.

"It's been two months. I can wait two seconds," Autumn said, sounding cheerful.

August picked up the pace, and once out of the parking lot and behind the church activity center building, August sat down and pulled the phone close to his mouth. His hands shook.

"Okay, Autumn, where are you?" August asked, praying for Fenton as the answer.

"Buffalo, New York." Like a boxer after getting punched, August tried to clear the cobwebs, even if the thought of his skin-showing-off sister in America's icebox amused him.

"What are you doing there?"

August waited ten seconds before repeating the question. He checked to make sure the call hadn't been dropped. "Autumn, I asked what are you doing in Buffalo?"

"Do you want to know what a high-school dropout girl with no skills does for work?" Cheerful Autumn gave way to the angry version. "Do you really want that image in your head?"

August remembered what she'd said on Christmas, but he needed to know.

"Yes, Autumn, you can tell me. I won't judge you and I won't tell anyone else."

"I'm working at a strip club." August heard no emotion in her voice, not excitement or embarrassment, speaking the words as casually as if she' said she was working at a strip mall dollar store. "I got a fake ID. That's all I want to say about it."

"What happened with Troy?"

"He lied. He didn't know anybody. I was his way to get out of Fenton. I thought I was using him, but it turned out the other way. I'd laugh except it would make me cry, so—"

"Autumn, why don't you come home? You don't want to do this."

Another long pause. August listened for sounds in the background. Loud music. On Easter Sunday. Who went to a strip club on Easter Sunday? "Autumn, you don't want—"

"No, I don't want to do this," Autumn said. "I need to do this. I need to make money."

"For what?" He heard her light up a smoke—that answered part of his question.

Autumn laughed. "Wow, you are an immature kid. I guess four months didn't change that." August thought it may have only been four months since Autumn left, but it felt like forever. Every day he stared into her empty room like the walls expected her home soon.

"Come home, then you don't need to do that."

"Look, August, I don't like the tone in your voice about this. This is what I do. Is it what I'll do forever? No. Is it what I want to be doing now? Not really, but my choices are limited."

"You could—" August started, but realized he didn't have any alternatives.

"I could do lots of things, but you know what? Shit happens," Autumn said. Inhaled. No doubt savored. Exhaled. "I used to read about famous people all the time in magazines like Us and People, about the crazy detours they had to make on the road to stardom." Another pause. August imagined her blowing smoke rings like so many hoops she'd have to get through in order to reach her dreams. His parents doubted them, as did he, but he wouldn't say a word.

August didn't read magazines. He'd rather have his nose in an eight hundred-page fantasy saga, never more so than now, for in that world there was a good and evil, right and wrong, nothing in the middle like Autumn described. "If that's what you need to do, little sister, I guess that's okay."

"Well, it's not the Pope's blessing, but it will do." Autumn laughed. August tried to soak in every second of the laugh so he could burn it in his memory. Maybe this laugh could take the place of the clicking sound of the empty gun pointed at someone and the trigger being pulled.

"Autumn, families can forgive everything."

"I hated the person I'd become in Fenton," Autumn said. Paused. Inhaled. Paused. Exhaled. "I'm not in love with this person I am now in Buffalo, but like I said, it's a stop on a road to someplace. All of this will make the movie about my life so interesting!"

August tried to laugh, but he couldn't fake it or force it. "So why did you call?"

"This morning, taking the bus to work, we passed a church as it was letting out. I just remembered one Easter us and church, you and me, Mom and Dad. I think I was nine. Amber was away at some camp, so it was just the four of us. It felt right. So I wanted to call."

"Thank you, Autumn. That means a lot."

"I wonder what happened to that little girl, and the answer is she grew up," Autumn said. "And I guess you have too now, knowing what you know about me."

"I wish I didn't."

"I'm not ashamed of what I do, and I don't want you to feel that way either."

August paused, unsure what to think, feel or know. He just knew he wanted his sister home, but if she couldn't be home then at least safe. "I could come out there and we could come back together. Walk hand in hand out of church again."

Autumn laughed. August felt embarrassed. "That's the spirit, August. Believe in happy endings. I know I do. And I know deep down I'll get mine. It's like that crappy karaoke song—Don't Stop Believing."

August felt the hot sun on his face, but it was tears, not sweat, trickling from his face. "Okay. For you, big sister, I'll believe in happy endings, although you coming home—"

"So let's end on that. I'm sorry I missed your birthday. Don't tell our parents we spoke, okay? It will be a brother and sister secret."

"You see, Autumn, that is halfway to a happy ending."

Another laugh from Autumn filled August's heart with the warmth of a thousand suns. "But I'll try to do better about staying in touch."

"That's all you need to do, just try to do better."

"Thanks, big brother."

"Thanks, little sister."

As soon as the call ended, August was online looking for the price of train tickets to Buffalo. He'd be like those heroes in those books. He'd rescue his sister and restore the kingdom of his family. Autumn was on her metaphorical journey while August researched for his real one. It seemed Autumn's descent began in earnest on homecoming, so August knew the only answer was for him to bring her home. Once he did that, then the two of them could walk in the door of their house in Fenton. There, together, August and Autumn would hear their father speak those three magic words, not "I love you" and certainly not "I hate you", but, "Welcome home, Autumn."

About the Author

Born in the same hometown as Michael Moore, Christopher Paul Curtis, and Jon Sczieska (Flint, Michigan), Jones started his writing career at age eight with an article for a New York City-based pro wrestling newsletter. Since that time he has published over two hundred book reviews, one hundred plus articles, fifty or so essays in reference works, nine professional books for teachers and librarians, seven young adult novels, and two nonfiction books. His current focus is reluctant YA readers with twenty titles published since 2013 with four due in fall 2015, and another four in spring 2016. Also in spring 2016, he will publish a nonfiction book for teens on changing the nature of teen incarceration.

He also teaches an online Young Adult Literature class at Metro State University in St. Paul, MN. Assignments in class are due on Tuesday mornings so he can watch professional wrestling on Monday nights. Some things change, some don't.

Patrick loves to hear from readers. You can find his contact information, website details author profile page at http://www.finch-books.com.

CPSIA information can be obtained
at www.ICGtesting.com
Printed in the USA
LVOW12s1626180416

484151LV00001B/82/P